THEN BEGGARS COULD RIDE

**Wildside Press Books
by Ray Faraday Nelson**

*Dog-Headed Death
The Ecolog
Then Beggars Could Ride
TimeQuest*

THEN BEGGARS COULD RIDE

by Ray Faraday Nelson

WILDSIDE PRESS
BERKELEY HEIGHTS • NEW JERSEY

THEN BEGGARS COULD RIDE

This book is copyright © 1976 by R. . Nelson. All rights reserved. No portion of this book may be reprinted without obtaining the prior written consent of the publisher, except for brief passages quoted for review purposes. or more information, contact: Wildside Press, P.O. Box 45, Gillette, NJ 07933-0045.

The cover design is by John Betancourt and is copyright © 2000 by Wildside Press.

irst Wildside Press edition: April 2000.

INTRODUCTION

Can we have Heaven on Earth without fossil fuels? And without nuclear energy? I think so, and this book is intended to show how, in a low-energy technology, we can fashion a world that is not only as good as our present world, but much better. It is in this sense I call it a utopia; it is not for mere mortals to fashion a world that is completely perfect. We are imperfect, therefore our imperfection will inevitably flaw anything we create.

Nevertheless, as I look around me at the society of the Sinister Seventies, I cannot help but feel restless and dissatisfied. Have we nothing to look forward to but more of the same, or something worse than this? Have we, indeed, passed the point of no return in some sort of plunge into universal oblivion? So we have been told, on appallingly good authority.

But I refuse to believe it!

I rebel against the doomsayers!

I seek to answer them, to show another way, and I draw my answer from a memory of my own life experience. There was a time when I, personally, had no car, no heaters, no electricity even; when I was so poor I found food by lurking in cafeterias—when patrons left their tables, I finished their leftovers. My clothing was hand-me-downs from friends, my shelter a condemned building where I lived rent-free, pending the coming of the wrecking crew. Was I unhappy?

No! I was perhaps happier than I have ever been, before or since. I had one natural resource that few people ever tap more than superficially; a resource that, unlike our supply of oil, coal and various metals, seems inexhaustible; a resource that grows greater rather than less as I use it.

I had my imagination.

My imagination made up for all I lacked.

As I sallied forth from my doomed dwelling place to perform my morning ablutions in the men's room of the corner gas station, as I wandered down to Telegraph Avenue to select a sumptuous repast from the groaning smorgasbord of leftovers habitually discarded by the American restaurant goer, as I sunned myself on the campus of the University of California and discussed philosophy with students and an occasional professor, was I a beggar? No. I never asked for money. Indeed, that summer (for this

Then Beggars Could Ride

life lasted only a few months) I neither accepted nor spent one single penny. Was I a bum? Was I a hobo, a beatnik, a hippie? (This was before Herb Caen coined the word "beatnik," back when a "hippie" was a sharp-dressing Black.)

I was none of these things.

Thanks to my omnipotent imagination, I was on Monday a monk, on Tuesday a troubadour, on Wednesday (having found the stump of a pencil and some discarded leaflets) a great artist, on Thursday a secret agent, on Friday a Zen Master, on Saturday a peripatetic philosopher, and on Sunday the Emperor of the World traveling incognito. Or I could be an explorer.... I did indeed explore the East Bay on foot, from East Oakland to the wilds of darkest Richmond. A composer, a dancer, a poet, a psychoanalyst, a naturalist, a swimmer, a runner, a clown; all these things I could be. I had but to imagine it, and it was so. And, as the occasion demanded, I was also a free babysitter, a free furniture mover, interior decorator, dishwasher, househusband (briefly), cook.

I knew a girl at that time, a student at Cal. She was
(A) in love with me,
(B) trying to reform me,
(C) both of the above
(D) or none of the above.

One day she asked me, "What if everyone acted like you?"

That is the seed of this book!

What if we lived in a world of make-believe, designed to the specifications of our fantasy, planned in our daydreams, molded to our heart's desire? What if we designed this world so you could live in any historical era, in any known place, or in times and places that never were, but only were imagined?

Could such a world be made possible? Could it be practical, stable, functional? Of course ... in the imagination.

But let's make the question harder.

Could it be possible *on a budget*? *In reality*?

Could it be possible with no technological breakthroughs, with no scientific knowledge beyond what we possess today? Could it be possible with no fossil fuels? (The day when we will be without fossil fuels approaches swiftly and relentlessly.) Could it be possible with no nuclear energy? (The problem of radioactive wastes has yet to be solved, and perhaps may be incapable of solution.) Could it be possible, not with impossibly good people, but with ordinary, flawed people like you and me?

I say yes!

Uptime from here, on one of the branches of possible futures, there is a world of make-believe made real. It's not far away. Come, let us join my protagonist as he seeks a home there. Perhaps we'll find your true homes there too.

I know mine is.

R. F. Nelson

PART ONE

CHAPTER 1

"Suicide, eh?"

"That's right."

The doctor, a short, thin, balding man in light blue business coveralls, stood with his back to me as he spoke, leafing through my dossier with an air of mild boredom. He raised his eyes to gaze out the circular window, his unimpressive body silhouetted against a bright cloudless afternoon sky, then turned to look at me for the first time.

"Light bothering you?" he asked.

"A little," I answered.

He grasped a handle at the window's rim and moved it, rotating the inner of the two panes of polaroid glass. The window went opaque and the illumination from the sun was replaced by a dim green shadowless glow from phosphorescent walls and ceiling.

"Better?" he asked.

"I guess so." I didn't really care, and my voice showed it.

"Won't you have a chair?" He gestured toward a simple but elegant piece of lightly stained flexible-wood furniture.

I sat down, remarking listlessly, "I was expecting you to ask me to lie down on a couch."

"No, no, that won't be necessary. I see that, like so many people who come to a therapist for the first time, you have a lot of false notions about us. This is the twenty-first century, not the nineteenth. I don't believe there's a single couch in this whole building."

"If you haven't got a couch, where am I going to lie down while you ask me about my childhood?"

"I'm not going to ask you about your childhood."

"What about my dreams?"

"I'm not going to ask you about your dreams, either."

A faint smile played about his lips as he seated himself behind his light elegant flexible-wood desk. "All those things have to do with your past. It's all here." He tapped my dossier with his finger. "But since your past has led you to attempt to kill yourself, you couldn't say it's been exactly good for you. No, we won't talk much about your past. It's your future that interests me, Jack."

"My name isn't Jack," I objected.

"I call all my male clients Jack, and all my female clients Jill. Later on you'll—"

Then Beggars Could Ride

"Just a minute there! I'm an individual! I demand—"

His sparse eyebrows shot up. "You demand your identity? It seems to me your identity was the very thing you wanted to be rid of when you took the pills."

"Touché," I said morosely. I didn't care all that much. "So my name is Jack. What's yours?"

"You can call me Doc." He stood up, leaned over the desk, and shook hands with me. As he sat down again, he went on, "As I was about to say, you won't be Jack forever. Someday, when you're ready, I'll hand you a list of names and say 'Pick one.'"

"What if I don't like any of them?"

"Then you can make up one. You can have any name you like with one exception."

"The name I was born with?"

"Exactly."

"Show me the list, Doc."

He shook his head, smiling wistfully. "Not yet."

"When?"

"In a year, two years. As long as it takes."

"That could be a long time. You could get as tired of me as . . . as I am of myself."

He rocked back in his chair and gazed up at the glowing ceiling. "Don't worry about that. There's something I think you ought to understand from the outset. We're not giving you all this free treatment out of charity, so you needn't feel guilty about it. We don't feel sorry for you. We feel . . . threatened by you."

I was astonished. "Why would anyone feel threatened by me?"

"The planet Earth has reached a certain kind of perfection, Jack. There's no war, no poverty, no starvation, almost no crime. The problems that terrified our grandfathers—air and water pollution, overpopulation, the energy shortage, racial and religious hatred, sexual inequality—they're all licked. People live a long time, and they're not sick very much. We have a utopia here, or as close as man has ever come to a utopia. So you can see that when you're so unhappy you'd rather have no life at all than a life among us, it causes, if not a threat to us, at least acute embarrassment." He looked at me expectantly, hopefully, almost pleadingly.

"You know," I said after a pause, "I never really thought about that."

I thought about it on the way home, as I pedaled my

bicycle along the elevated bikeway, filling my lungs with clean, fresh, flower-scented air. I looked toward the San Francisco Bay, where the sun was setting behind the triple-decked Golden Gate Bridge; saw all the vertical windmills rising from rooftops and backyards and rotating slowly in the breeze like huge barrels with two broad slits in their sides; saw the seven and eight story business-buildings, one wall covered with a vast curving parabolic reflector that focused a powerful stream of sunlight into a facing "target building"; saw the other bowl-shaped solar collectors dotting the skyline; saw the homes all built at a certain angle to the sun and painted in a certain combination of black and white paint that regulated winter and summer temperatures without the use of heaters or air conditioners; saw the small farm-parks that separated the blocks of homes and business structures at regular intervals; saw the almost noiseless electric trucks entering and leaving the auto level of the freeway beneath me; saw the duroplastic rain canopy above me.

It was all perfect, except for me.

"It's a good mim," I told her.

It was indeed a good mimicry of a knee-length white satin flapper dress from the late nineteen-twenties. Marge pirouetted coquettishly, showing off the dress (and her silk stockings), then struck a pose, one slender hand touching her short peroxide-blond hair, the other raising skyward a cigarette in a long ivory cigarette holder. I had to admit my wife was very much "in period," very authentic. The flapper style was perfect for her, with her small boyish figure. (I did not look nearly so convincing in a coonskin coat.) The final touch: she was vigorously chewing gum. Through the gum she said, in a pleased voice, "Aren't I the bee's knees?"

"Yes."

"Say it, Newton!" she commanded me.

"You're the bee's knees, dear."

She stopped posing, fairly well satisfied, though I knew she would rather I'd call her "Sweetie" or at least "Baby." "Dear" wasn't the best possible mim for her period, though I'm sure there were people in the twenties that called each other "dear."

"In fact," I added, hoping to please her," "I might go so far as to say you're the cat's pajamas."

"Now you're talkin'!" She gave me a light kiss on the

chin, then took me by the hand and led me into the front room. The front room, of course, was decorated in a rigorous Art Deco style, all metal, glass and simple geometrical forms. The whole apartment was Art Deco. Indeed the whole neighborhood was Art Deco. I had occasionally pointed out that no real neighborhood in the twenties was completely Art Deco. To be a genuine mim, our street would have had to have had at least one or two buildings from some previous era. Whenever I pointed this out to Marge she would reply, "Who would live in them?"

Which was logical. If someone wanted to live in a house from some non-deco period, they would not set up housekeeping here in the Chaplin District.

"What'll ya have? The usual?" she demanded, stepping behind the rectangular bright red bar.

"Nothing, thanks."

She raised a painted eyebrow. "Nothing? Say, are you turning prohibitionist on me?" The Chaplin district played at prohibition, but was not really dry, as were some more ruralist twenties neighborhoods.

"You can have something if you like," I said.

"I don't like to drink alone. You know that. Now how about it?" She opened an unmarked bottle and poured two shot glasses of bathtub gin. I caught a glimpse of myself in the wall-to-wall mirror behind her. I was too thin, too pale, too sick-looking, almost a walking skeleton.

"No, thanks," I said.

"But you *always* have a drink when you come home."

"A man can change."

Now she was getting angry. "I like you the way you were."

"The way I was was suicidal. Did you like that?"

"Hey, buster! What are you up to now? Are you trying to put the blame on me? It was you, not me, that tossed those sleeping pills down your throat. I was the one that held your head while you vomited them up. I was the one that called the doctor. Damn you, Newton. . . ." Here she calmed herself, with visible effort, before continuing, in a coaxing, seductive voice, "Let's forget about that, honey. We both need a drink."

I turned away from her and went over to the picture window. It was dark outside, except for the illumination in some of the neighbors' windows. I saw my own gaunt reflection again, this time double, on the inside and outside panes of the double window, and for some reason I thought, *This window's not a perfect mim. There weren't any vacuum-gap insulating windows in the twenties.*

Marge came out from behind the bar. I could see her reflection in the window, but dared not look at her directly. Did I think I'd turn to stone? Her next remark caught me off guard.

"Why don't you go to the bathroom, Newton?"

"What?"

"Why don't you go to the bathroom? Did you go to the bathroom at that doctor's office?"

"Well . . . I suppose I did. What difference does that—"

"I knew it! Don't blame me if you have to eat your supper cold!"

I sighed and shrugged noncommittally. Our gas stove burned methane produced in the basement septic tank. But I was sure there was no shortage of sewage.

"Can't a man call his soul his own?" I demanded, somewhat inanely.

"You can have your lousy soul! But your *excrement*—" She pronounced this word with an appalling French accent, in a tone of infinite disgust. "Your *excrement* belongs to your family!"

I stared dumbfounded at her retreating image in the reflection as she made her theatrical exit into the dining room. She did not want me to change. Therefore she did not want me to go to the doctor. Not ever again. She loved me for my own sweet self-destructive self.

Would I go to the doctor again?

A panic voice somewhere in the back of my mind cried out, *You must!*

I went over to the bar.

Both shot glasses of gin still sat there on the counter top, untouched. She had left them there for me.

I perched on one of the two high bar stools, gazing at the shot glasses for several minutes, before at last selecting the one on the right and raising it in a mocking toast to my cadaverous reflection in the mirror.

"To us," I whispered, then tossed off the gin in a single swallow.

It tasted awful. I coughed, shook my head, wiped my watering eyes with my sleeve, then, after a deep sigh, reached a bony hand for the other shot glass.

SUPPER was late.

It was, of course, my fault. If I hadn't gone to that silly

Then Beggars Could Ride

doctor, we would have eaten before nightfall as usual. We would not have had to burn all the electric lights in the dining room and kitchen. We would not have had to waste precious electricity stored in the apartment batteries by ever-so-many rotations of the windmill on the apartment house roof. I thought of suggesting that we dine by candlelight, but I dared not speak. The family would have noticed the tell-tale slur in my speech. Did they already smell the gin on my breath? There was no telling. They were all too polite to mention it; besides, there was nothing worthy of comment about my being, as Marge put it, "a wee bit squiffy." It was normal, even expected.

But I had been to the doctor.

I had said, "A man can change."

That was worse, even, then the fact I'd tried to kill myself. Suicide was some sort of obscure venereal disease, unmentionable perhaps, but curable. But to change oneself ... that was treason!

"Pass the meatballs to your father, Ruth," commanded Marge.

Ruth, a redheaded teenager, but otherwise a carbon copy of her flapper mother, obeyed.

It was not Sunday, but we were having meat, though meat is ever-so-much more expensive than other, more vegetable, sources of protein, ever-so-much more wasteful of energy, of Mother Earth's not-unlimited bounty.

But it had been decided, long ago, that I loved meat. Whenever we ate meat, so the story went, it was to give Daddy a treat. Actually I didn't care what I ate. Meatballs or seaweed-flour mush . . . it was all the same to me.

I ate a lot, showing my gratitude.

I burped jovially.

Marge gave me a pained smile, but I knew she was pleased.

The others smiled too: pretty young Ruth and my mother-in-law, Doris Whittle (who often referred to me as "that spineless jellyfish"), and my father-in-law, Wilber Whittle, who rarely said anything at all. How forgiving they all were! How Christian!

"I love to see a man eat," Mrs. Whittle remarked. "And you could certainly stand to put a little meat on your bones." She had more than a little meat on hers; her white "Russian peasant" blouse, which should have hung loosely around her body, was filled to the exploding point with her immense, almost frightening, breasts. Whenever she reached for another helping, I listened hopefully for the sound of ripping cloth.

Mr. Whittle made no comment. He was almost as thin as I, but shorter . . . shorter, in fact, than Ruth; he was the shortest and lightest of us all. I wondered, for the millionth time, how he managed to resist his wife's force-feeding.

"Won't you have some ice cream?" Mrs. Whittle asked me sweetly.

"No, thanks," I answered.

"Are you sure?"

"I'm full up. It was such a fine meal."

"All your favorite foods."

"Yes, I noticed."

"Well, I'll have some." Mrs. Whittle helped herself to the ice cream, her pudgy paw holding the dishing spoon delicately, little pinkie extended.

"I'm going out tonight," Marge announced offhandedly.

"The church again?" her mother asked her in a pleased voice. (I never went to church.)

"That's right," Marge said, dabbing her lips with her napkin so her words were slightly distorted. "We have to practise, you know."

"Is it *Fifty Million Frenchmen* your theater group is performing this year?" Mrs. Whittle asked vaguely.

"No, silly," Ruth answered, getting up from the table. "It's *Wake Up and Dream*."

Mrs. Whittle nodded, satisfied. "I knew it was one of those Cole Porter things." It was always one of those Cole Porter things.

Marge made her exit, humming "What Is This Thing Called Love?"

Mrs. Whittle turned to me. "Maybe you can get caught up on your work," she said primly.

"Maybe I can," I said, pushing my chair from the table.

"You must have fallen behind," she added, frowning.

I stood up. "Yes, I suppose so." I thought, *Suicide is so time consuming.*

WITH the best of intentions, I seated myself at my L-shaped chrome-legged glass-topped desk in my closet-sized office just off my bedroom. (Marge and I had separate bedrooms.) There, on the transparent desk top, sat my automatic telephone-answering machine, waiting to tell me who had phoned me during the week since I had botched my melodramatic but ultimately rather disgusting death scene;

Then Beggars Could Ride

waiting to plunge me once again into the "real world" of advertising.

The telephone-answering machine was not a mim of the twenties. It made no attempt to pass itself off as one. It was there, not as part of the period decor, but as a frankly functional reminder that we were not really in the twenties after all. In the twenties office workers went to work. Human bodies were transported over highways to offices. Now electrical impulses were transported over wires, and nearly all office workers worked at home. A human body, not to mention the vehicle carrying it, has so much more mass than an electrical impulse.

I looked at the machine for a long time.

My hand, when I thought about reaching for the "on" switch, had a great deal of mass.

Was Marge right? She thought I should quit working for a company outside the community. She felt my work cut me off, prevented me joining in the fun, prevented me from really believing, as she claimed she did, that Warren Harding was president. If I worked in the community, perhaps at the local newspaper. . . .

I fished a copy of the local newspaper from the wastebasket.

The Chaplin Republican.

It was, at first glance, a good mim. The headlines and national news were all from the twenties. The local news, on the inside pages, was relentlessly trivial though about real present-time events—chamber of commerce meetings, the Elks, churches. The mim wore thin only when one tried to rip the paper. It would not rip. Nor would it burn, or turn yellow. The paper was almost eternal. The print, however, was another story. It was already beginning to fade, as it was supposed to. By the end of the month, when the boy with the wagon came to pick it up and take it back to the newspaper office for reprinting, every page would be completely blank.

If one wished to make an enduring mark in the world, *The Chaplin Republican* was not the place to make it.

I was about to return the paper to the wastebasket when I realized Marge would be angry. One didn't put newspapers in the wastebasket. Someone only had to take them out again.

I carefully laid *The Chaplin Republican* on my desk.

Only people who will not be here tomorrow (and I thought I would not be when I first put the paper there)

put newspapers in wastebaskets. What did one put in wastebaskets? Hardly anything. But they helped the mim.
No mim was ever perfect, but all of them tried.
Marge worked in a so-called "sweat-shop" a few blocks from here, a very authentic sweat-shop at first glance, but unlike the sweat-shops of the twenties, it was never either very hot nor very cold. Though it used foot-treadle sewing machines, nobody ever really sweated.
It wasn't authentic, but the majority of the lathes, drills, sanders and other small machines in the nearby machine shops were also operated by foot-treadle.
I got up, paced the narrow room, turned on the radio.
The radio was a mim, too, actually a five-channel loudspeaker. Its signals arrived, not through the air, but through a cable from the local "radio station." Four of the channels played transcriptions of old twenties records and radio shows; the fifth channel gave real local news. There was no real national or international news.
"And now, live and direct from the fabulous Aragon Ballroom," came a thin crackling voice. Was that right? Wasn't the Aragon Ballroom later? In the thirties?
The band began playing the Charleston (or a mim of it).
Too loud. I turned it down almost to a murmur. Background music.
I sat down again. I said, out loud, "It's all so unreal!"
Of course nobody answered.
I contemplated the telephone-answering machine. If I wanted reality, it would have to come from that little gadget, the only thing in the room with no pretentions.
I leaned forward, switched it on. Work would get my feet on the ground. Work would snap me out of this rotten mood.
The first voice on the tape recording was that of my boss, George Garvey. "Heard about your trouble," said the gruff, good-natured voice. I tried to picture him. I'd never met him face to face in all the years I'd worked for him. He lived in San Francisco, on the other side of the bay. I could have pedaled across the bridge, but what for? "You been workin' too hard, kid." He always called me kid. "Why don't you take a month off? I'll put Mrs. Puttnam on your accounts."
"No!" I shouted, bringing my fist down on the desk top with a crash.
The voice went on unperturbed, as recorded voices always do. "Take care of yourself, kid. Don't worry about a

Then Beggars Could Ride

thing. Then, maybe in a month, maybe in two, call in and we'll get you going again." Suddenly the voice hardened. "But don't call in before that, and don't call in until you got your head on straight. You hear me?" The voice softened again. "Goodbye, kid. Take care of yourself."

A click, then silence.

There was nothing else on the tape.

I punched keys, tried to contact some of the other ad men. I got the lock signal. They weren't accepting calls from my number. On impulse I keyed in the area code for Dallas, Texas, and tried to ring up the company central computer. The lock signal. Even the computer wasn't talking to me.

That shook me up. I should have expected it, but it was a complete surprise. Who wants to talk to a suicide? Even a computer draws the line somewhere.

But with no computer there would be no computer games. Dallas had a great simulation of Star Trek spacewar in its program banks, right out of the Sinister Seventies. And some fine gambling games.

I felt like smashing the telephone, but controlled myself. *I need a drink*, I thought.

The telephone regarded me with a perfectly blank screen. I could phone anywhere in Chaplin, I knew, but not outside. No digital readout. No facsimile printouts from the world's libraries. No television! All that was now *in the future*!

I wondered, with irony, if maybe Warren Harding really was president, and got thirstier and thirstier.

THE street, as I walked briskly along the sidewalk, was tree-lined, quiet, and dimly lit. There were cars parked along the curb, mims of Fords, Chevies, even a Reo Flying Cloud, huge under the streetlight, and square, its maroon paint job polished so it gleamed. *Was that right? Wasn't the Flying Cloud later?*

What did it matter? They were too clean to be good mims; and they had electric motors under the hood, if they had any motors at all. Mere status symbols!

The street was a fake in other ways too.

Where, for instance, were the gangsters, the muggers, the stickup men? The street was too safe! How could a criminal operate in a community where everyone knew everyone else and where, if he did pull off some sort of crime, he'd have to escape on foot, on a bicycle, or in a car that couldn't go more than thirty-five miles per hour and that, if it did manage to leave the community, would look like a time machine anywhere else?

I was alone. There was not another soul in sight down any of the cross streets. A clear sky. The moon almost full. Plenty of stars. Everyone was asleep. Everyone was missing this. Except maybe my wife and her friends, singing Cole Porter songs at the church far off to my left. (I stopped a moment to see if I could hear them, but I couldn't.)

How phony it all was! How totally phony!

I needed a drink. That, at least, would be real.

I began running.

The Chaplin community, like all the communities in the Bay Area (or the world, for all I knew then), was hexagonal, with the farming areas and bikeways and roads at the rim, and the factories, stores, restaurants and public buildings clustered around a little park in the center. It was toward this center I was loping.

To an outsider it would have appeared that nothing was open in the central business district, but I knew better. I knew where there was a speakeasy.

I turned down an alley, knocked at a basement door.

A tiny window opened; a pair of suspicious eyes peered out.

"Joe sent me," I said. (I could have said almost anything and still gotten in.)

The door opened. Panting, sweating, I stumbled in and threw myself into a chair. The dixieland band was playing the final bars of the "St. Louis Blues." The spotlight turned on them was the only bright light in the room. On the tables, clustered around a narrow dance floor, flickering candles were stuck in the necks of empty wine bottles. Very dim. Very smoky. Some might even say very romantic.

The musicians filed off the bandstand. Trumpet, trombone, clarinet, saxophone, tuba, drummer, and banjo. They all wore straw hats and garters around their sleeves. (Was that right? Garters?)

A fat negress in a low-cut, red-sequined gown sat down at the piano and began softly playing, "You Were Meant for Me." She had been here many times before when I'd dropped in for a drink, but this was the first time I'd really paid any attention to her though, as I now noticed, she played like a real big timer.

"What'll ya have?" demanded a scantily dressed waitress

Then Beggars Could Ride

in a high squeaky voice. I looked up, startled. She was chewing gum. "What'll ya have, big boy?" she repeated.

"Whiskey sour," I muttered.

"Comin' right up," squeaked the waitress over her shoulder as she minced off toward the bar.

I smiled at the lady piano player.

She smiled back.

I got up and went over to speak to her. She was fat, yes, but sexy all the same. "Hey, Daddy, what's happening?" she greeted me, still playing.

"I don't know. Nothing much. Nothing ever happens around here."

She raised an eyebrow. "Plenty of action, baby, if you know where to look for it."

"Maybe you're right. I guess it's me there's something wrong with."

"If there's something wrong with you, change it," she advised cheerfully.

Another optimist, I thought angrily. "Oh yeah? Then why don't you change yourself into a white woman?"

She went on playing. "I gonna tell you somethin', child. Only you keep it to yourself. I *was* a white woman once."

"What?" I blinked down at her stupidly.

"Thas right," she said firmly. "I was a white woman, living in a mim of the eighteenth century . . . eighteenth-century England. . . . an' one day I come by this community on the bikeway, an' I heard some music playin', an' fell plumb in love with it. The doctors did a good job on me: a l'il plastic surgery, a l'il repigmentation in my skin, a year or so of training, and here I is!" She had a deep, self-satisfied chuckle.

I didn't know whether to believe her or not, though it was certainly possible, so I said noncommittally, "Those doctors are pretty smart."

She cocked her head to one side and asked, "You been fixed?"

"Fixed?" Now what was she talking about?

"You know. You got you vasectomy operation? You sterilization operation?"

"No. I only have one daughter."

"Ain't made you quota yet, eh?" Every couple was allowed two children, no more.

"No."

"I ain't fixed neither. An' don't wanna try makin' mah

quota tonight. Too bad, honey." She flashed me a wistful grin.

"Yeah, too bad."

I went back to my table, where the waitress was delivering my drink.

As I drank it I listened to the piano music. The phrasing was too perfect, too tight, like a minuet. I decided that she was probably telling the truth.

WHEN I came shuffling and weaving out of the alley I still didn't feel like going home. *Going home to what?* I asked myself.

The Palace Theater across the street was dark, but as I got closer I could hear faint gunfire and music. According to the marquee, there was a double feature playing tonight (as usual): *Wings*, starring Clara Bow and Gary Cooper, and *In Old Arizona*, with Warner Baxter as the Cisco Kid.

Plus selected shorts. All for a quarter.

I kept on going. The movie was probably almost over.

I left the central business district and headed out through the light industrial area, then the residential area, but I was careful to avoid my own part of town. I didn't want to meet Marge and her church friends as they came home from the rehearsal. It wasn't long before I found myself at the rim of the hexagon, next to the gate that led out into the farming area. I had been here many times before; several times a year everyone in Chaplin, man, woman and child, pitched in to help with the agricultural work for a week or two.

I entered the farming area, shuffling aimlessly along.

Here were the big compost drums, looming above me in the semi-darkness. I placed my hand on the metal side of one of them; it was warm to the touch. The garbage and sludge inside it were "working." I thought, *Marge was wrong*. My excrement didn't belong to my family, but to the whole community. How nice to know that I was able to make some contribution to my neighbors' welfare!

I grasped the big wheel on the side of the frame in which the compost drum hung. *What harm would it do to turn this drum over?* (The drum hung in an upright position, its top high above my head, its bottom about at eye-level, so it could be easily dumped.)

"Not that one," came a deep voice from behind me.

I turned, startled. Out of the shadows stepped a mus-

Then Beggars Could Ride

cular, middle-aged oriental in the white fiberglass coveralls of the Tech Department. "Well, hi there," I said, flustered.

He gestured toward the compost drum I had been touching, saying offhandedly, "I turned that one already, about an hour ago. There are still a few along here that need turning and watering, if you want to help."

"Okay," I said. I didn't have anything better to do.

Together we inverted five big compost drums in their support frames, unsealing the top of each in turn and watering it down with garden hoses, then sealing it up again. (The drums opened both top and bottom.)

"Don't mind the smell, do you?" he asked.

"No, I'm not crazy about it, but. . . ." Compost never bothered me. The smell seemed rather pleasant, actually, if the drum was inverted regularly, wetted down and "working."

"How come you're working at night?" I asked him.

"This is when the job needs doing."

"Do you get overtime pay for night work?"

"Nope."

"But your union—"

"Techs don't have a union."

I didn't know that before, and it surprised me. "How come?" I demanded.

"We techs," he said, grinning, "we're not the workers. We're the bosses."

I puzzled over that as we strolled toward a crop area. "I don't understand," I said finally.

"Someday you will," he answered, then added, "or maybe you won't." He unsnapped the plastic canopy on a wheeled trough of seedlings, turned to me and said softly, "You interested in plants?"

"Sure," I lied.

He lifted the lid and snapped on his flashlight. "Have to open the canopies once in a while to change the air. Plants breathe, you know, like you and me." His voice had fallen to a reverent whisper. "These little rascals are going to be tomato vines. There's potatoes under the soil, but you can't see 'em. Now look sharp for bugs."

"I don't see any."

"The plastic canopy mostly keeps them out, but you can't be too careful." He was closing the canopy now and snapping shut the seal. "Keeps the water in, too, and lets us control exactly the composition of the loam. You know it takes only a small fraction of the water to grow a tomato plant in a box, compared to what it would take out in the open. No evaporation, you see, and no water sinking down too deep for the roots to get it. Since we got into the habit of getting the plants up off the ground and in sealed boxes, we can grow things anywhere, even in the middle of a desert."

We moved along briskly, not opening every box, but only spot-checking here and there, as he explained things— how they could get three or four crops a year from a plant that in a natural environment would produce only one, how they deliberately left some plants to the bugs. "No bugs, no birds," as he put it. But it wasn't the bugs and the birds that interested me. It was him.

"Do you get paid a lot?" I asked him as we moved a wheeled container shaped like a coffin into a shed. (He claimed the plants in it were getting too much sun.)

"Not a lot," he answered.

"Then why do you work so hard? I mean, even at night."

He spoke very seriously now. "I think I'd pay them to let me do this job."

He seemed to expect me to understand, but I didn't.

"How much longer will you work?" I asked.

"I'm about finished."

"Going home?"

"Sure. Of course. And what about you?"

"I think I'll hang around here a while," I said.

He looked at me with suspicion, as if he thought I might be planning some spectacular act of vandalism on his beloved plants, then he shrugged and said, "Suit yourself. Good night."

"Good night."

He walked away in the direction of the Chaplin residential area, not looking back. If anything was messed up, I guess he thought he'd know who to blame.

I continued on through the dim, shadowy farming area, passing row on row of orange trees, each in its own wheeled pot, each covered with a loose, crinkly transparent plastic bag. There was a vague idea in my mind of getting as far away as possible from Marge, but then I came to the edge of the farming area.

There was a wire fence, and beyond the wire fence the divided pavement of the truckway, unlit and deserted under the continuing canopy of the bikeway above.

I was about to turn back when I saw, on the other

Then Beggars Could Ride

side of the truckway, a sudden flash of fireworks in the sky. An instant later there was a sputter of pops and bangs as the sound reached my ears. To my surprise, I heard what could only be distant music.

I wondered, *What's happening over there?*

I realized with a shock that I'd never in my life been on the other side of the truckway, and if I'd ever glanced in that direction from the bikeway, I couldn't remember what, if anything, I'd seen.

The other side of the truckway was a land of mystery, as unknown and inviting as ancient Atlantis. One thing was certain; it was not at all like Chaplin!

In an instant I scrambled over the wire fence and was running, weaving slightly from side to side, across the truckway.

CHAPTER 2

"Well," asked Doc, "what did you find on the other side of the truckway?"

"Chinatown!" I answered with disgust.

He had, out of consideration for me, darkened the round polaroid window of his office, and we were bathed once again in the submarine glow of his phosphorescent walls and ceiling. He crossed the room with a quick, light step and examined a map of the Bay Area hanging near the door. Sitting, as before, next to his desk, I followed his movements with my eyes.

"Here's your enclave." He pointed. "And right next to it—yes, this must be it—we find a mim of China under the Ming dynasty. The Ming dynasty is a period noted for scholarly and artistic achievements, you know."

"Oh?"

"Yes indeed. For some Chinese, it's the best of all Good Old Days."

"They did seem to be having a lot of fun," I admitted. "Fireworks, parades, masks, and that earsplitting music." I groaned.

"Did you enjoy yourself, Jack?"

"What do you think?" I grumbled. "I couldn't understand a word anyone said, and they couldn't understand me either."

"So what did you do?"

"I went home of course."

"Weren't you curious? I mean, here you were, discovering a whole new world almost on your doorstep. Didn't you feel an urge to explore, to observe more?"

"I told you, I went home. It was a mistake to cross the truckway in the first place."

He turned to face me, eyes glittering with suppressed excitement. "But you *did* cross. That's a sign of progress."

"Why?" I challenged.

"Did you know the—as you call it—Chinatown was there, before you crossed the truckway?"

"Well, no. I guess not."

"But you must have seen it many times as you passed it on the bikeway."

"I didn't pay any attention."

"Until now," he corrected me, then turned again to the map. "You come here from your enclave on your bike,

Then Beggars Could Ride

don't you?" I nodded as he glanced my way. "You must pass along this elevated bikeway." His forefinger traced a path on the map. "You must look down into ten, maybe twelve different communities. Each community is a mim of a different time and place. Identify them for me, Jack."

"I can't!"

"Identify one."

I searched my memory wildly. There were jumbled images in my mind of buildings, solar mirrors, windmills, the farming areas that separated one community from another, but nothing I could pin down to a particular time and place. Suddenly, without warning, that feeling I call "Black Ecstasy" swept over me, the feeling of total helplessness, the feeling of living in a universe so overpowering that suicide is the one positive act possible. The last time I'd felt this way, I'd taken the pills. I closed my eyes.

"Stop!" he shouted. Startled, I opened my eyes again. The dark vortex faded but did not vanish. It never vanished completely. It was always there, coaxing me, whispering to me of my helplessness, my failure, my slavery, telling me I was a victim of fate, of the stars, of society, of history.

"What are you feeling right now?" he demanded, taking a step toward me.

"Leave me alone." I was surprised to find I could hardly speak.

"What are you feeling?" he repeated harshly.

"Rotten," I whispered, but as I spoke I began to feel better.

Doc's voice softened. "This is the same feeling you had when you tried to kill yourself." There was no uncertainty in his voice, and I knew he was right. For the first time, he impressed me. "There's a kind of darkness around you, a mental darkness, isn't there?"

"Yes, how did you know?"

"I remember," he said softly. "Where you are now, I once was myself."

And yet, I marveled, *now you are a doc, a tech*.

"You've never really looked at that darkness before, any more than you've looked at the communities you passed on the bikeway," he added gently, and once again he was right.

"Are you saying I'm crazy?"

"No, normal. It's normal to look at things without seeing them. Most people are in a kind of hypnotic trance at all times. Negative hallucination—failure to see things that are there—is the most normal thing in the world. Psychotherapy itself, up until the breakthroughs of the 1990s, suffered from a negative hallucination, which they called the subconscious mind. There are ways, now, for breaking out of negative hallucination, ways we've learned, not from studying the mentally ill, but from studying the more-than-well, the creative minority, what were once called geniuses."

"But how?"

"Leonardo DaVinci said it. 'Only the trained eye really sees.'"

Doc taught me some mental exercises, so simple they seemed stupid. I agreed to do them, to do them regularly, because something somewhere inside me seemed to be saying, "That's right. That's right."

Was it that this elementary training was already having an effect? I saw, as I pedaled away from the mental health center, that it and all the buildings and grounds around it were not a mim of anything at all. Like the buildings in the farming areas, these structures were simple, functional, almost ugly in their total lack of style.

I not only saw this, for the first time, but I understood what it meant.

The techs live in real time, and they are the only ones who do.

As I continued down the bikeway, I made a special point of identifying the time and place of each community I passed.

UNEMPLOYED!

Is there any other word in any language quite so seductive, luxurious, delicious?

I was getting disability checks, having convinced some computer somewhere of my psychological imbalance, and Marge was working a full eight hours at the so-called sweat shop. For years I had thought the sky would fall if I quit working. Actually life moved along only too well without me.

For a week I spent most of my time at the public library. I had thought there would be nothing particularly helpful there, just "escape literature," but I was wrong. Though there was nothing on the shelves with a later copyright date than 1929, I uncovered the roots of modern society.

In the books I found, there was information about

Then Beggars Could Ride

a curious Victorian Era artistic-literary movement called the Pre-Raphaelite Brotherhood. Dante Gabriel Rossetti was one of the early leaders; William Morris was one of the later. In their painting, poetry, fantasy-fiction, architecture, furniture design, handicrafts and lives, they strove to ignore the industrial revolution, then in full swing around them, and live as much as possible as if the renaissance had never happened. When Morris organized a business, it imitated a medieval guild in many respects. When Morris organized some of the earliest socialist organizations, it was on medieval models. The Marxists condemned Morris's efforts as "utopian"; "Utopian Socialism," which expressed itself in small experimental colonies, was eclipsed by Marxian Socialism, which expressed itself in violent revolution.

But Utopian Socialism did not become completely extinct. A law student named Auston Lewis studied the works of Morris, then moved from England to the United States—to San Francisco, to be exact. There Lewis became a leading figure in a California movement that included, as its most famous member, Jack London.

Jack London built a castle called Wolf House on a farm modeled on a Medieval barony. The castle was burned down before he could move in; some say it was an act of arson by Jack London's Marxist rivals. Jack London died of poison soon after. Some say it was suicide; some, murder by the same men who burned the castle. At my regular Thursday afternoon session with Doc, I proudly recited the results of my research.

He leaned back in his chair, smiling approvingly, and said, "Good work, Jack. Of course the story doesn't end there, though."

"That's as far as I could trace it in a library from the twenties." I was pacing the floor excitedly, no longer the apathetic, suicidal figure I had been during the previous session. "What happened next?"

He templed his fingers reflectively. "Through the thirties, forties, and fifties Utopian Socialism led an almost subliminal existence, but never completely died out, particularly in California. People who had never heard of the Pre-Raphaelites or Utopian Socialism were, all the same, influenced by the basic idea of creating small utopian communities that voluntarily isolated themselves from the so-called 'modern world.' There was Henry Miller and his group, and after that the Beatniks, then the Hippies."

"How's that?" I'd never heard of any of these groups before.

"They were all a certain kind of bohemian, aiming to refute the cliché, 'You can't turn back the clock.' "

"There must have been others," I said.

He gestured toward a photo on the wall of a man in front of a streamlined train.

"There was Walt Disney, of course, but his Disneyland, though two-thirds devoted to reproducing the physical appearance of the Victorian Era, was not a true mim, since nobody actually lived in it. There were other fairs in the same spirit—Dickens Christmas Fairs and Renaissance Pleasure Faires—which annually recreated on a limited scale various bygone eras but fell short of being true mims. And there was the Society for Creative Anachronism, whose knightly tournaments were held at intervals all year round, and whose members often wore the costumes of the Middle Ages even in their daily lives. These partial mims served two important functions: they prepared the public for the true mims that came later on, and they kept alive and brought to a high degree of skill the handicraft technologies of the past."

"Go on! Go on!"

He smiled at my impatience.

"It was the nineteen-seventies that, viewed in retrospect, were the turning point in history," he said, choosing his words carefully. "In the Sinister Seventies the movement toward racial and ethnic integration ground to a halt and reversed itself. The Blacks, the Chicanos, the Chinese-Americans, the Jews, the American Indians, the southern Whites all refused flatly to allow their cultural, linguistic and historical identities to be melted down in the Melting Pot, refused to move out of their ghettos, refused to be reduced to a colorless national common denominator. To the dismay of well-meaning reformers, other, formerly dormant minorities, such as the various immigrant communities in the big cities, instantly began asserting their separateness." He paused to chuckle, then added, "There was a lot of folk dancing in the seventies." He glanced at me with a calculating eye. "You don't find this boring, do you, Jack?"

"Of course not! It's like a whole new world opening up to me. Why didn't anyone tell me?"

"You didn't ask." He was grinning at me in the ghostly green light. "But let me continue. There were other forces in play in the seventies. It was an era of secrets. In China a chain of abortive violent revolutions took place in secret. The United States fought whole wars without the knowledge and consent of the majority of the American people. A few super-rich families waged a no-holds-barred struggle for control of the U.S. presidency that lasted for generations but was hardly suspected by the average citizen. Secret agents made secret agreements. Secret weapons were tested in secret laboratories. I tell you, to this day historians are still peeling away one layer of secrecy after another off that era. But there was a price to pay. The public gradually lost faith in the national government. Toward the end of the seventies, nobody believed a word the president and national government said.

"Then came 1980, the Year of the Great Cold. The world was totally unprepared, though the weather had been getting colder every year since the forties; there were terrible panics. Crank pseudo-scientists proclaimed the dawn of a new ice age and were almost universally believed. The national government, quite rightly, laid the blame for the Great Cold on sunspots and, quite rightly, predicted that in the years following the world would warm up again, but were almost universally disbelieved. Before the year was up, there were no more national governments.

"The Communist countries were expecting a breakup of the West, but their Marxist prophecies failed to warn them that they too would be caught up in the universal collapse." He sighed and shook his head sadly. "There was a lot of bloodshed, needless bloodshed. There was, one might say, a Third World War, but it was not fought on a grand scale in one place. It was like a free-for-all, small-scale violence everywhere, as the enclaves of ethnic and racial minorities, freed from supervision by a national authority, went for each other's throats. It was a bad time, a very bad time.

"But out of it, during the last decades of the twentieth century, gradually evolved the world we live in today, the world of the mim enclaves. When I was a boy, we were all obsessed with nostalgia for some bygone day of half-real, half-imagined glory. That, I think, was the moving force that drove us to build the mims. But now everything works so well we simply accept it."

"Some of us don't accept it," I said softly.

He stood up, frowning. "True. Very true. But you are feeling better now, aren't you?"

I hesitated. "Yes, I suppose so."

"Are you doing the mental exercises I taught you?"

"Well . . . sometimes."

He shrugged. "But not regularly, eh? Never mind. These historical studies you're getting into are much more important. Modern psychotherapy, you see, is concerned, not with the Self, but with the World."

Abruptly, the session was ended.

"WHERE did you get that thing?"

Marge was referring to my sombrero.

"El Cerrito," I told her, cocking the hat at a jaunty angle.

"What's El Cerrito?"

"A little town in California . . . California as it was under Mexican rule."

"What were you doing there?"

"Exploring."

"And what happened to your shoes?" She had finally noticed I was barefoot.

"I traded them for the hat."

"You're insane, Newton." Under her makeup she had turned quite pale. "You're finally, actually insane. I don't know about you, but I need a drink!" She led the way to the small home bar in our front room, where she poured two shot glasses of gin. She drank hers at a gulp and waited for me to drink mine.

"Well?" she said impatiently.

"I'll pass," I said.

"Don't tell me that, Sweetie. I know you. As soon as I leave the room, you'll chuggalug it."

"No, I won't." My voice was calm, a little distant.

"You will!"

"No I won't."

"I don't understand you anymore. You're a stranger to me, Newton. I'm living with a stranger! Are you trying to drive me to suicide? Trying to make me kill myself in your place? It won't happen, Sweetie. I won't let it. You know women live longer than men. It's a law of nature."

"You make our relationship sound like some sort of endurance race."

"Isn't that what marriage is all about, Newton? A contest to see who can live longest?"

I was not angry, as I might have been only a few weeks earlier. When she said I was a stranger, she was right.

Then Beggars Could Ride

I looked at her, watched her mouth opening and closing and making words, and all I could think of was, *You're so small, Marge. So small.*

She was talking at me as she headed for the door, then she was gone. She'd left my drink for me. She was certain I'd pick up the glass, drain the familiar bad-tasting poison.

I smiled and went to my room, leaving the glass and the gin within it untouched.

EARLY one Sunday morning I was pedaling along the elevated bikeway, far from home, having gotten up before dawn and slipped out without waking the family, when I caught my first glimpse of the ships. I got off my bike and stood for a long time by the railing, looking across the maze of rooftops and windmills at the distant forest of masts and rigging. Except for an occasional church bell, the enclaves were silent, awesomely silent, under a cloudless sky. I was alone on the bikeway. There was nobody around to embarrass me with a curious glance, so I prolonged the moment shamelessly, sipping it slowly.

Finally I mounted my bike and continued on, heading toward the ships as directly as the hexagonal network of bikeways permitted. It took less than an hour to reach the docks.

There I dismounted, leaned my bike against a warehouse wall, stumbled forward along the pier, gawking like a tourist. There were few people around, and they paid no attention to me, though some seagulls, perched above me on the yardarms of the vessels, squawked hopeful demands for food at me.

The ships were beautiful.

No wonder they were a favorite subject for painters, even painters who had never seen a ship! Most were three-masted clipper ships, long and slender and graceful, the final result of a centuries-long evolution. They rose and fell gently, rocking so slightly they hardly seemed to move at all, moving only enough to let you know they were afloat, and now and then one would bump the pier with a muffled thump and a scrape. I read the nameplates on their prows, all in ornate brightly painted Victorian lettering. *The Ariel. The Taiping. The Serica. The Fiery Cross.* And there was *The Cutty Sark!*

Last in line was the longest of them all, *The Flying Dutchman*, with a coat of fresh green paint.

Suddenly I noticed a man on the *Dutchman*, leaning on

the rail and looking down at me. He had been so still I hadn't seen him before; now he was only a few yards away. For the first time it occurred to me I might be trespassing.

"Hello," I said awkwardly.

"And a good morning to you, sir," he answered, apparently amused by my discomfort. "I see by your clothes you're a visitor here." (I was wearing a white sweater, white slacks and white tennis shoes.)

"I'm from uptime, in the twenties. A little place called Chaplin."

He nodded. "I've been there once or twice. Wouldn't like to live there, though."

"Why not?" I was only a little offended.

"Wouldn't like to live in any one place steady, but if I had to live in one place, it'd be downtime. Imperial Rome or something like that. Uptime is fine for the womenfolk, but downtime favors us men." He chuckled to himself.

He was wearing a dark navy-blue peacoat like an ordinary sailor, but the visored cap on the back of his head indicated he was an officer, perhaps the captain of the *Flying Dutchman*. He was thin, deeply tanned and, judging from the tufts of white hair around his ears, about fifty years old. His expression was wise and kindly, with a suggestion of strong character despite the schoolmasterish steel-rim spectacles perched on his nose.

"My name is Newton McClintok," I said.

"I'm Captain Marlinspike Werner, sir, and if you'll come aboard, I'll shake your hand." He gestured toward the gangplank.

The handshake, when I joined him on the foredeck, was a rough and hearty one, and afterward he looked at me teasingly, saying, "It's a soft hand you've got there, Mr. McClintok. I was going to ask you to join my crew, but now I wonder if you're man enough for the job."

"The last thing I'm looking for is a job," I told him lightly.

"But you might like to do a tour of my ship, eh? Have a look around?"

"Well, yes, I would, Captain Werner."

"Come along them." He led the way. "And by the way, you can call me Cap Marlinspike. I like the sound of that name."

Amidships I said, "She's a good mim, Cap."

Then Beggars Could Ride

"A good mim! She's perfect!"

"I notice a windmill on the bow."

"Yes, well, I need power for my radio and electronic navigation gear, don't I?" When I laughed he added, "Think that's funny, do you? There's worse to come, and I might as well tell you and get it over with. The hull looks like wood, doesn't it?"

"Yes, of course."

"It's actually fiberglass reinforced with steel. And why not, eh? Fiberglass is light and strong, and it don't rot or rust, and it's easy to patch. Why not, I say! And you might think my sails are canvas. Not on your life. They're Dacron, sir, and my lines—what you'd call ropes—they're not made of hemp, but nylon, like a whore's panties!"

"The whole ship is plastic then?" I couldn't keep the disillusionment out of my voice.

"That's right, sir. You could say that. Plastic is the Great Pretender. It can look like anything, and it can do anything, and the rot and rust and mildew and salt water and sea creatures leave it alone. There's more to a ship than being a good mim, you know. We don't sit in a museum somewhere. We go to sea. And while we may be joking around, the sea is always dead serious. We need every advantage we can get." He started down a stairway leading belowdecks.

"Why bother with sail at all?" I asked, following him down out of the sunlight. "Why not make her a steamship and get it over with, if you don't care about making a good mim?"

It was dark in the passageway. We had to feel our way along. "Steamships pollute, Mr. McClintok. If the techs saw smoke coming out of my ship, they'd put me ashore for good. And what would we burn, eh? Oil, coal? All fossil fuels are used as a part of plastics and chemicals and things. They've become far too rare and expensive to burn." We stopped by a porthole. He tapped it with his knuckles. "See? The porthole has plastic instead of glass, doesn't crack as easy. That's where your coal and oil goes these days, into things that last a while."

We continued on down the passageway. I said, "What I mean is, if a good mim doesn't matter, isn't a sailing ship kind of inefficient?"

"Inefficient?" He was indignant. "There's nothing more efficient than a sailing ship! We can sail for years without an ounce of fuel. Perpetual motion! What could be more efficient than that? The inefficient thing is to carry fuel along with you, taking up space where you could be putting paying cargo." His voice took on a more confidential tone. "It's my opinion, sir, that even without all this fuss about mims, the sailing ship would have made a comeback. The rising price of fuel makes it absolutely inevitable. The sailing ship is better than the motor ship in every way but one. It's not as fast." We stepped into the deserted crew's mess and walked between the long tables. He added, "But we ain't so crazy about speed as our grandparents were. These days, if someone is going to travel at all, he wants to take his time about it."

The last place Captain Marlinspike Werner showed me was his own cabin, in the stern right under the afterdeck. Except for some sophisticated radio equipment that peeped from behind a half-drawn curtain, this room was a more perfect mim than anything else I'd seen on the ship.

It looked exactly, and I mean exactly, like a captain's cabin must have looked in the Late Victorian Era. The stiff formal black and white photo of—I suppose—his mother and father; the flowery wallpaper; the massive ornate dark-wood table and chairs; the rolltop desk; the built-in bunk; the scarf across the table decorated by a picture of Windsor Castle; the pitcher and washbasin on the dresser; the small cabinet beside the bunk containing, no doubt, a chamber pot; all these things combined to produce an overpowering impression of nineteenth-century elegance.

I sank into a chair, awestruck in spite of myself. The captain smiled proudly, expecting a compliment.

But I couldn't bring myself to praise this room, or his ship, or his way of life. The Black Ecstasy, which had left me alone most of the time lately, now came on me suddenly, in full force. What good was all this? What was the point of it all?

I tried to frame a sentence that would convey some meaning, yet not offend the old seaman. "Listen, Captain Marlinspike."

"Yes, sir?"

"Don't you ever long for a little . . . progress?"

"Progress?" He looked at me almost with pity. "No, sir! No, indeed! It's not efficient."

"Progress is not efficient?" I was dumbfounded.

"Of course not. Why, take this ship, for example. It cost me plenty, I assure you. If there was progress I'd

Then Beggars Could Ride

sail it a few years and then it would be obsolete. I'd have to junk it! It'd still be perfectly seaworthy, but I'd have to junk it. Is that efficient? But as things are, without progress, I can go on sailing her until the day I die, and then some other fellow can sail her all his life, and then some other fellow. Don't you see? The initial cost of *The Flying Dutchman* can be amortized over *all eternity!*"

CHAPTER 3

"Shall I darken the window?" Doc asked, silhouetted against its circle of bright afternoon sky.

I answered, "No, I don't mind the light."

He smiled. "How symbolic."

I smiled. "If you say so."

He crossed to his desk and sat down. I was already seated. Our eyes were on the same level . . . perhaps that was symbolic, too, of our growing equality. But of course he had the window behind him, while I had the door. This was his turf, and I was only a visitor.

After a thoughtful pause, he began, "I get the impression there is a great deal more light in your life than there was when you first came here."

"Maybe so."

"Don't tell me maybe!" His voice was suddenly sharp, almost angry. "Is it yes or is it no? Decide!"

I laughed nervously. "It's yes."

"No more drinking?"

"Not a drop."

"Is your wife still bossing you around?"

"No, and that upsets her."

"Be as gentle as you can, Jack. I've looked at her file and . . . well, it would be a shame if you graduated from this office only to have her take your place."

"Don't worry. She's all right. She's a tough broad. Nothing can get her down for long."

He frowned and said, "You still have your blind spots, it seems. But on the whole, you've been getting out? Visiting other enclaves?"

"I'll say! Wait 'til you hear—"

"Generally speaking, would you say you feel better?"

"Sure, but I don't understand why. I mean, you're not doing anything. You just sit there."

"There is sitting and sitting," he answered enigmatically. "There is acting and acting. I am trained to create large effects with small causes, like the Frenchman who permanently changed the ecology of California by importing and releasing two snails. But tell me, have you had any more spells of what you call Black Ecstasy?"

I hesitated, then admitted, "Yes, while I was talking to an old sea captain." I recounted the conversation with Captain Marlinspike, ending with, "He said the techs could

Then Beggars Could Ride

put him ashore if his ship made smoke. Is that true?"

He nodded. "Yes."

"Then you techs have some sort of police power?"

"Yes."

"Then how is it that I never heard of that power?"

Doc tried to hide it, but I could tell he was not happy with the line I was taking. "We almost never have to use our power."

"If someone kills his wife—"

"We leave that to the local authorities."

"A thief—"

"No concern of ours."

"Rape?"

"None of our business."

"Then what?"

"All the traditional concerns of law and morality are matters of cultural taste, different in different enclaves, dependent on what time and place the enclave mims. We police only crimes that really matter, crimes against the survival of mankind. These do not often occur, thanks to people like you."

"Like me?" That was a surprise.

"You were an advertising man, weren't you? You know then that advertising doesn't really sell products, but images, images of life roles. People like you, under our direction, sell the public role-images that make anti-survival actions—quite literally—unthinkable."

"But some people—not many, but some—aren't swayed by advertising. What do you do then?"

"Let's say a man builds a factory that pollutes a certain river. We shut him down."

"What if he resists? What if he's rich and powerful?"

Doc chose his words with care. "You must understand that no matter how rich or powerful he is, he does not have at his disposal the technology, particularly the weapons technology, of today. Only we techs have that."

So now we see them. The teeth!

"Let's take another example," I said.

"Are you sure this is the best use of your time? There are other questions."

"Another example!" I insisted.

"Allright. Let us say a woman has more than two children. We check the situation in her enclave. Usually the birthrate is low enough so the extra children can be absorbed into the community, in which case all we do is insist she undergo a sterilization operation. Accidents and what little disease that remains in our society makes it possible for us to absorb slightly more than two children per woman . . . let's say, two and one tenth."

He looked as if he'd like to change the subject, but I pressed him. "But what if you find the community already has too many children?"

"Then we take the extra children from her and put them up for adoption. There are always a certain number of childless couples."

"But let's say there's a child nobody wants to adopt. What do you do then?"

Doc sighed deeply, and his answer, when it came, was full of regret.

"We kill it."

THE following morning, as I pedaled along the sunny elevated bikeway, I meditated on some of the subtleties of Doc's remarks. (I was becoming very sensitive to subtleties, perhaps hypersensitive.) Doc had mentioned that I had been an advertising man. The past tense! In other words, I was not now and would not in the future be an advertising man. The decision had been made without my knowledge and consent, by person or persons unknown. But it was only logical. If I was going to be a different person, wouldn't I have a different profession? Of course. I was a fool not to realize that at once!

The other subtlety was the matter of the killing of the unwanted child. Doc had seemed reluctant to talk about it, but *it had been he who brought it up*! Was there a lesson in there, intended for me? Of course.

If an unwanted child can be killed, so can an unwanted adult . . . like myself.

The conclusion?

I was being prepared for something, but I had no idea what. I did know, however, that if these preparations failed, it could mean my death.

I surprised myself with a burst of dizzy fearful anger.

The therapy, if it was supposed to cure me of suicidal tendencies, was obviously working. A few weeks ago I wouldn't have cared.

My wanderings that day carried me farther south and higher in the hills than ever before; I often found myself shifting down into the lower gears and, once or twice, was

Then Beggars Could Ride

forced to dismount and proceed on foot, pushing my bicycle beside me.

It was as I was plodding up one of these steep grades and had almost reached the top of the rise that I saw the Mormon temple. I was approaching New Deseret, one of the most famous enclaves in the Bay Area and one of the few communities nearly everyone, regardless of the period of their mim, knew at least something about. This temple, which lifted its curious tower above the trees like some alien spaceship, had been built long before the Great Cold, though the enclave of New Deseret had been founded during the years of confusion that ended the twentieth century.

New Deseret's fame was not so much a result of anything done here, but because of the remarkable story of the Mormons' founding of Salt Lake City, Utah, way back in 1847. Salt Lake City was a pioneering settlement in more ways than one; though not really a mim, it was probably the first successful enclave—in the sense of a community that separated itself from the larger society—in the United States, though some give the credit to the Amish. (The Amish originated in Europe.) New Deseret was a mim of Salt Lake City, more or less, but not the Salt Lake City that actually was. It was Salt Lake City as it should have been.

A few moments later I coasted down a brief offramp and braked to a stop before New Deseret's impressive massive pink marble entrance, with its ponderous redwood gates four times as tall as a man. Though the big gates were shut, a small gate to my right was open. Pushing my bike, I strolled toward it.

Just inside the door, in the shadowy interior of the wall, there were bike racks. I hesitated before leaving my bicycle there, but an amused voice called out from behind me, "Don't worry. Your bike will be safe. There is no stealing in New Deseret."

As I rolled my bike into place, a man in coveralls and an ample beard came toward me. I could not see him clearly, since my eyes had not yet adjusted, but he seemed friendly enough.

"Are you a church member?" he asked me.

"No."

"I see." For a moment he seemed a good deal less friendly but he quickly recovered his hospitable manner. "Well, visitors are always welcome to the outer areas."

"Outer areas?"

"You didn't expect to be allowed to come barging right into our lives, did you?"

I turned away from him, ready to leave. He put his hand on my arm. "Stay, brother," he said softly, then called, "Jacob!"

Another bearded man in coveralls came through a low doorway on the opposite side of the room. "Show this fellow around, will you?" said the first man.

Jacob shook hands with me and asked my name and home enclave. When I had answered he led me back the way he had come into a sunlit, palm-lined courtyard. I noticed, above the wider doorway nearby, an inscription:

> Lay out your cities, but not so large that you cannot readily raze the whole city should an enemy come upon you.
> Brigham Young

I gestured toward the carved letters. "What enemy are you talking about?" I was wondering if it was me.

"We've had our share of enemies," Jacob said, still walking, not looking at me.

"But that's all in the past, when your people practised polygamy."

"We practise polygamy now."

"Really? Isn't one wife enough? More than enough?"

"One bad wife is more than enough. One cannot have too many good wives."

"Good wives?"

"Obedient ones."

"You don't say." The idea of an obedient wife seemed to me almost a contradiction in terms. I hung back a moment, then had to run a few steps to catch up as Jacob started up a flight of stone steps.

"Jacob," I said, following him up the stairs. "Give me a tip, will you? How do you get a wife to be obedient?"

"I obey God. Do you have a disobedient wife?"

"Well yes."

"If you obey God, your wife will learn to respect you and obey you."

We had reached the head of the stairs and found ourselves on a wall overlooking a clean, busy, prosperous-looking city, somewhat in the style of the Old West. I was instantly struck by the absence of women.

Then Beggars Could Ride

"Jacob! Where are the women?"

"At home."

"But the shopkeepers, the schoolteachers, the . . . the women in all the other professions?"

"There is one profession for a woman, the profession of wife."

I was about to protest, then thought better of it. I had what might be called a liberated marriage, but was I happy? I said mildly, "Do your women accept that?"

He nodded solemnly. "Those who do not accept it are free to leave. Some do leave, but they always come back."

"They do?" My tone was one of frank disbelief. "Why?"

"I think they would rather share a strong honest man than have a weak liar to themselves."

I looked out over the city. It was unlike Chaplin in that it had the farming areas and residential areas mixed instead of separate, probably to give a better mim. The effect was one of green coolness, simplicity, naturalness. I felt strangely attracted to it.

I blurted, "Could I come and live here?"

"If you become a Mormon," he answered.

"Could I marry a Mormon woman?"

"Of course."

And, I thought, *if I was already married, it wouldn't matter here.*

Before leaving, I got Jacob to give me copies of the Mormon sacred books, *The Book of Mormon* and *The Code of New Deseret*.

As I mounted my bike, Jacob said, "I'll be seeing you."

I pedaled home slowly, by a roundabout route, thinking.

The sun was setting as I coasted down the offramp into Chaplin, but still I did not go directly home. The night was warm. Why not ride around a bit?

That's how I happened to pass by the mouth of the alley next to the "sweatshop" where Marge worked. That's how I happened to glance down the alley and see Marge in the arms of a muscular, somewhat balding man. She was kissing and being kissed. Her back was to me, so she did not see me.

It was only a glimpse I caught, in the glow that lingered after the sun had gone, then the momentum of the bicycle carried me on. A glimpse was enough, however, to throw my mind into almost complete paralysis.

I parked my bike in the little park at the center of town and sat down on a bench.

"Well, I'll be damned," I whispered finally.
I'd have to do something, but what?
I made a firm decision.
I would do . . . nothing.

Doc sat behind his desk, fingers templed. He had not darkened the window. I sat in front of the desk, looking down at my shoes. (I was wearing my white tennis shoes, along with my white slacks and sweater.)

He asked, "When you found out what your wife was up to, did you get drunk?"

"No," I answered quietly.

"That's good. But did you feel like drinking?"

"Not a bit."

"Perhaps you began plotting some frightful revenge?"

"No."

"It's not good to hate someone and keep it all bottled up."

'I don't hate anyone."

"You must feel something toward this man who is having an affair with your wife!"

"Yes, I do feel something," I said timidly.

"What do you feel?"

"Gratitude."

He burst out laughing, then inquired, "Why gratitude?"

"This other man . . . maybe he'll take my place . . . if I go away."

THERE came a soft knock at my bedroom door.

"Come in, Marge," I called. (Who but she would visit me in the middle of the night like this?)

It wasn't Marge. My massive mother-in-law entered quickly and closed the door behind her with care. Annoyed, I threw on my bathrobe.

"Really, Mrs. Whittle. . . ." I began.

Fingertip to lips, she silenced me, then whispered, "Son?" This was probably the first time she'd ever called me son. "Son? Can I talk to you?"

"Tomorrow perhaps."

"No, now."

We were standing, facing each other. It occurred to me that if I did not offer her a chair, she might leave. I asked her, "What's wrong?" but kept my voice cold and hostile.

She glanced furtively around, little pig eyes blinking rapidly, avoiding my gaze. "Son? Are you all right?"

Then Beggars Could Ride

I straightened, proud of the weight I'd put on, proud of my healthy suntan. "Never better, Mrs. Whittle!"

"No, I mean mentally."

I shrugged. "Can one ever know that about oneself? If I am insane, I'm enjoying it."

"You're not yourself."

"What do you mean?"

"You're riding around on your bicycle all the time, but you never tell us where you've been. Why are you doing this to us, son?"

"I'm not doing anything to you."

"You're pulling away from us, abandoning us. Don't leave us!" Her pudgy fingers gripped my arm with surprising strength. I looked at her, standing there in her wide white peasant skirt and overstuffed peasant blouse. I was delighted to note that I did not feel guilty.

"Please, Mrs. Whittle."

"Is it another woman?"

I laughed. "No, nothing like that."

"If it was, we'd understand. Mr. Whittle . . . well . . . I've had a few things to forgive him for."

"Really?" This was news to me. I felt a new respect for the old man.

"If it's not a woman, what is it? Where do you go? What do you do?"

"I visited Chinatown, a sailing ship, various enclaves—"

"There must be more than that!"

I shook my head. "No, that's all."

"Are you angry with Marge for something?"

"No."

"Be honest!"

"Nothing."

"You can talk to me. I can keep a secret."

"There's nothing to tell."

Frustrated, she turned toward the door. "You don't trust me. I'm your friend. I cook all your favorite foods. But you don't trust me." Abruptly she faced me again. "If there was something to forgive Marge for, you'd forgive her, wouldn't you?" she demanded.

I didn't answer.

Mrs. Whittle left, closing the door carefully, noiselessly.

CHAPTER 4

Doc looked up from the papers on his desk. Behind him, through his circular window, I could see storm clouds gathering in the afternoon sky. His narrow face was in shadow, his small thin hands restless. The back lighting on his balding head glowed in his sparse unruly hair like a halo.

"Well, Jack." He paused.

His light blue business coveralls were unzipped at the neck, a response to the high temperature and muggy moist humidity. Heat and lightning flickered in the clouds behind him, but there was no thunder that I could hear.

"Well, Jack," he began again, rustling his papers. It disturbed me somewhat to see him unsure of himself. "Have you made your choice?"

"What choice?"

"Your choice of a place to live. Did you think you could become a new man without living in a new place?"

It was obvious now that he pointed it out. I asked, "But my wife, can I take her along?"

He sighed. "She would remember the old you, cling to the old habit patterns."

"I see."

It was much hotter and damper outside, but the building, which had no air conditioner, gave a good deal of protection from the weather. It was, like everything else, not perfect; only as perfect as considerations of energy conservation would allow. This therapy—if it could be called therapy—was not perfect either; only as perfect as man's imperfect knowledge would allow. "You'll have to leave her, but you would have left her if you'd killed yourself, you know. This way it will not be quite as cruel. She'll know you're alive, though she won't know where," he said gently.

"Can I write her a letter?"

"It would be unwise . . . counterproductive."

Was I surprised? No. I had known and not known all this for a long time. The knowledge in one part of my mind had been hidden from the rest by that old familiar mental fog. Doc called it "mog," and said that it was Man's greatest enemy: an enemy so cunning only a few of its victims were aware it was there. If it were ever once defeated, all other enemies would be almost helpless, all problems, by comparison, childishly easy to solve. But I had to admit that, with Doc's help, I was managing to drive the mog back, at least a little way.

"Have you been doing your mental exercises?" he asked.

"Sometimes."

"You should do them regularly, every day."

"I forget."

"The mog makes you forget."

Beyond his shadowed head the storm clouds were moving toward me, rolling, changing. There were clouds in my mind, too. It was the inside weather that mattered. "I'll try to do better," I promised.

"Now!" he said abruptly. "What are you thinking?"

"Huh? What?" I was confused, suddenly sleepy. In my mind, rapidly vanishing like a half-remembered dream, was the image of a child's corpse, broken, bleeding. Or was it a midget? The face was so old and wrinkled.

It was my face.

I said, "I'm thinking about myself, as a child, dying."

"Don't let it get you." Doc was smiling. "It's a common image for people at this stage of therapy."

"What does it mean? That I'm going to die?"

"You are not going to die, Jack, but maybe as a child, you will."

I felt a sudden anger. "That's what you think!"

He nodded. "Yes, that's what I think. A child is innocent. Of course he is. But why? Because he is helpless. He can do nothing wrong because he can do nothing at all. But give him power. Give him a real choice that can change his life and the lives of others; then he's innocent no longer. Whatever happens, good or bad, is his fault, not the fault of the stars, or his parents, or society, or history, or fate. There's a secret truth at the heart of the lie that power corrupts. Power is choice, with the risk of failure and guilt, but without choice you can never grow up. Our society provides a range of choice that is greater than any previous society, as great as the limitations of being human permit. I ask you again, have you made your choice?"

I thought of the Mormons, the Mexican-Americans, the Chinese, the ship. The mog rushed in, mixing them together, flashing me a hundred images of other enclaves, other mims. How many different enclaves were there? How could I choose one and thus reject all the others, with their infinite range of possible experiences?

My head ached. I closed my eyes with a moan, leaned forward until I was bent double.

Through the mog came Doc's voice. "You need not choose yet."

The mog receded. I sat up, feeling better. "When?"

"That's up to you."

I felt better yet. "You're saying I have forever?"

He shook his head sadly. "No, not forever. If, after a reasonable period of time, it seems you are not going to make up your mind at all, I'll have to decide to . . . terminate your treatment." He looked so unhappy as he said this that I felt sorry for him, but the feeling of sympathy did not completely overcome the other feeling.

Fear.

As I pedaled up the on-ramp to the bikeway, the storm hit. Only the first drops of rain managed to strike me before I reached the shelter of the canopy. I stopped there and got off my bicycle to admire the violence of the downpour.

I was dry on my side of the bikeway, but on the other the rain slanted in and quickly formed shallow puddles on the pavement. At my back, as I leaned against the bikeway railing, was the medical center from which I had come; ahead of me, beyond the opposite railing, was a stretch of farming area, then an enclave, Ancient Greek or Roman from the look of it. The red tile roofs of the homes slanted inward, collecting the rain and pouring it through a rectangular hole in the center into a cistern below. This way of building roofs, like so many Greco-Roman architectural ideas, was so logical (or should I say ecological?) I wondered briefly why anyone would do things any other way.

The temperature had dropped rapidly; in a few minutes excessive heat had given way to a definite chill. Nonetheless the bikeway was quite crowded, or perhaps only seemed that way since everyone was moving along on the same side of the road, avoiding the rain.

Several bicycles passed, then a boy on roller skates, a pair of joggers, and a rickshaw containing an old Chinese gentleman who nodded at me as if he knew me, though I didn't recognize him.

Then, at the lower end of the onramp, in the Greco-Roman enclave, appeared a sedan chair containing a fat, effeminate fellow in tunic, toga and sandals. It was a disturbing sight, but it was a moment before I realized why.

Then Beggars Could Ride

The four strong naked men who carried the sedan chair must be slaves!

But how could that be? In a world where one could be whatever one liked, why would anyone choose to be a slave? Then I remembered that the Mormon had told me women who left New Deseret always came back, though his explanation of why had not really satisfied me. If women could choose to be wives under a system of polygamy, why couldn't men choose to be slaves?

The fat man shouted something in Latin and the slaves broke into a run, making his belly and double chins bounce. The slaves were smiling.

What was it to be a slave, to choose deliberately to be a slave? *To choose not to choose!* And I understood. Freedom is a heavy burden. For most people, it is heavier than the fattest Roman. Is it any wonder, then, that when it is available some people prefer bondage? The mog in my mind seemed to be saying, *Who will live longer? The healthy slaves or the sickly, worried master?*

The sedan chair passed close by me. I got a good look at both slaves and master, and indeed the slaves looked better than the master. Their faces were handsome, open, though a little blank. His was furrowed with tension, gray with the strain of too many decisions.

The Roman was heading in the direction I had intended to go, toward Chaplin. On impulse (was it some kind of momentary panic?) I set off in the opposite direction, pedaling so hard I soon overtook the other bicyclists who had gone by me a few moments before.

I did not look down into any of the enclaves I passed. Each would have been one more choice, reaching out its claws for me. Perhaps it was carelessness. Perhaps it was mog. Anyway, when I finally came to a stop, I hadn't the least idea where I was. Thanks to the rain, I couldn't even tell north from south.

ONE thing was certain; I was nowhere near home.

The signs at intersections were in every language but English, nor were there any English-speaking people among the few passersby I asked directions from, and the darker the sky, the fewer passersby there were.

Until then I had not realized how dependent I was on distant landmarks in my wanderings—the bay, the hills, the Golden Gate Bridge—not realized what would happen if these landmarks were obscured. What could I do? Wander aimlessly up one bikeway and down another all night long? I'd catch pneumonia!

Better to take a chance and seek shelter in some strange enclave picked at random. On foot, wheeling my bicycle, I started down an offramp in the near-total darkness, feeling my way along as the full force of the storm exploded in my face, drenching me to the skin.

I knew, because I was bumping into compost drums and large terrariums, that I was passing through the farming area, and I briefly considered crawling under one of the broader terrariums and dagging my bike in after me, then realized that might shelter me from the rain, but not from the wind and the cold. I pushed on, maintaining my direction (I hoped) by feeling my way along what seemed to be a main aisle.

Ah, there, up ahead, was a light!

I moved more quickly, sure now that I was going toward the residential area. The light, which was a good deal higher than my head, vanished, but I kept on in the same direction, and a moment later bumped into a smooth, featureless wall.

I felt my way along the wall for some distance to the left, then finding neither window nor door, I felt my way an even greater distance to the right. There was no trace of an entrance of any kind.

I began shouting for help.

For a long time there was no answer, then, from somewhere above me, a gruff voice called something in a language I did not recognize.

With a scrape and a thump something was lowered beside me. I reached out, groping, and grasped it, finding it to be a crude wooden ladder, so crude its rungs were secured with leather thongs. Abandoning my bicycle, ignoring the ladder's apparent state of collapse, I scrambled upward.

I AWOKE slowly, and with the coming of consciousness came a sense of guilt. For the first time in my life I had stayed out all night. Marge would be worried sick.

Or maybe, I reflected, she wouldn't be.

Either way I should try to find a videophone and give her a call, then ask directions. But then I remembered that I was in a mim of a Hopi Indian pueblo. There were no videophones in Hopi pueblos, not even the crudest sort of crank telephone. And how could anyone give me directions if I couldn't understand a word they said?

I kept my eyes closed, unwilling to begin the day.

Last night was a vague scramble in my mind . . . the climb up the rickety ladder, the meeting with the gruff-voiced man who led me indoors—thank God—out of the storm and into the firelight, the man who had turned out to be, from the look of his pajama-like clothing, sweatband, broad dark face and black hair and eyes, a Hopi Indian.

He'd given me dry clothes like his own, given me a mat stuffed with straw to lie on and a beautifully woven blanket to keep me warm, and I'd fallen asleep almost instantly, without a thought for the worry I might be causing my family.

I listened for the sound of the storm, but there was silence. Perhaps the storm had passed. The air in the room was comfortably warm, though I couldn't hear the crackle of the fire in the fireplace. There was a smell of smoke in my nostrils, but it was old smoke. I wondered what time of day it was. Morning? Afternoon? Evening?

I opened my eyes.

An old Indian woman was crouching on her haunches at the foot of my bed, absolutely motionless. Our eyes met for a long moment, then she arose and quickly left the room, without even attempting to speak to me.

I sat up, yawned, stretched and scratched myself.

There were no windows in the little room, but enough light came through the doorway so that I could make out my surroundings. There were several other mats like mine on the floor, a pile of Indian blankets, some earthenware pots with beautiful geometrical designs on them in bright primary colors, a loom and, in a place of honor, on a sort of altar, three brightly-colored wooden dolls decorated with feathers. The dolls were vaguely human in shape, but highly abstract in design, as much like animals as men really. They were, as I knew from some of the duller classes in High School, Kachina dolls, images of the Hopi gods.

The old woman reappeared in the doorway, accompanied by another Indian, a lean old man in the usual Hopi pajamas, but adorned with a great deal of finely wrought metal jewelry. (Was that real silver?) His movements were not those of the old man he appeared to be, but quick and graceful, like those of a young athlete or dancer. He murmured something to the woman, and she left.

He sat down on the floor beside my bed and regarded me gravely. When at last he spoke, I was surprised to find that he spoke English, though with an odd accent. "Have you come to join us?" he asked.

I had not expected such directness. "I ... I don't know," I stammered.

He nodded slowly. "Then it is chance that has brought you here?"

"I suppose so. But anyway I don't see how I could join you. I'm not an Indian."

"Nor was I when I came here, but now I am what you would call a medicine man, a leader in this enclave."

"But how?" I now knew about re-pigmentation and cultural training, but this man seemed so Indian he was almost a stereotype.

"Was Hitler a German? Was Napoleon a Frenchman? I was born Black, but science and what you would call Hopi magic has transformed me."

"Black?" I rubbed my eyes. "Why would a Black want to become a Hopi?"

"I see you, like most Whites, know little of the history of other races. You do not know that the Hopi, together with other Pueblo Indians, are perhaps the only colored people in the United States ever to win a war against the white man. You do not know how, in 1680 we drove out the Spaniards and kept them out until 1692. We, known to all other tribes as the 'Peaceful People,' won for ourselves twelve precious years of freedom. It is those twelve years we live and relive in this enclave. Those twelve years are our Golden Age. And the man who led the Indians in that war was Popé of San Juan, a medicine man like me." There was pride in his voice, though his face remained impassive.

"I see," I said. "So you identified with the oppressed. . . ."

"You would identify with the Spaniards, of course. You are white. You've never been oppressed."

"Well, I wouldn't say that—"

He waved aside my feeble objections. "So chance, not desire, has brought you to the enclave of Kiva. But what is chance, eh? What is it but the will of the Great Kachinas?" He glanced at the stylized befeathered dolls on the altar. "Or it may even be that you are one of the Great Kachinas in disguise. If men can wear the masks of gods, cannot gods wear the masks of men?"

Then Beggars Could Ride

He looked at me keenly, expectantly, as if waiting for an answer worthy of one of his gods, but I couldn't think of a stupid answer, let alone one glowing with cosmic wisdom.

To see men as gods—and demons—in disguise seemed insane. In our mim it would be regarded as a common symptom of paranoid schizophrenia. In the enclave of Kiva, however, it was I who was abnormal, crazy. At that moment I glimpsed for the first time the further reaches of the vast freedom the enclaves offered, a freedom not bounded even by the limitations of sanity. No matter how much of a misfit one might be, there was someplace on the planet where one would fit in and be "normal."

He rose to his feet. "Then come, white man, and see our microcosm!"

I followed him out into the sunlight. From the position of the sun, I judged it must be almost noon. There were still some cumulonimbus clouds on the horizon, dark and glowering, but the storm had passed. I saw the Bay and was no longer lost.

I COULD have left then and gone home, but I didn't.

Instead I followed, fascinated, as the medicine man led me on a guided tour of the enclave of Kiva.

Kiva was located high in the Oakland hills, within sight of the Mormon temple. The Kiva pueblos were terraced structures, almost like step-pyramids, built of stone and adobe . . . but the outer face of the adobe was surfaced with a hard plastic that protected it from the weather. I soon learned why I'd been unable to find any doors and windows on the ground level; there were none. The doors and windows began on the second floor, so that even though there were no real Spanish soldiers due to attack, the pueblos were much like forts.

The farming area was almost identical with the one in Chaplin, except that the crops were all traditional Indian foods such as maize, beans, mim, squash etc. The medicine man explained that here a mim was impossible; ancient Indian agricultural methods were too dependent on the whims of the Rain Kachina. The tribe was not willing to undergo periods of famine simply to preserve the ways of the ancestors. The area, rather large, devoted to sheep herding, did seem quite authentic, until I stopped to wonder if the Indians, back in 1680, had any sheep. I asked my guide. He didn't know.

We went up one ladder and down another, crossed roofs that were, in their turn, porches for higher dwellings. We saw weavers at work on large figure-eight looms, potters working without potters' wheels (this at least was "in period"), women in long cloaks feeding children, and still we climbed higher. I could not believe simple pueblos could be built so high, and asked the medicine man about it. He offhandedly informed me that the walls were reinforced with steel girders.

Late in the afternoon I met the medicine man's adopted father and mother—had supper with them in fact. The medicine man was an old man, though in vigorous health. How old could his adopted parents be? I asked him.

"Father is ninety-seven. Mother is a hundred-and-two."

They smiled at me with, I'm sure, their own teeth, slightly yellow but all there.

"It is not unusual for people of our tribe to live to be a hundred and fifty," said the medicine man. "We do not smoke, drink alcohol, eat sugar, use drugs. We work hard in the open. Most of all, we do not worry. We know the Kachinas will take care of us."

We were squatting on low stools in a room in one of the lower parts of the pueblo, eating "piki," a strange bread that looked like blue tissue paper. The piki looked revolting but tasted rather good, as did the odd vegetable dishes that came with it. I paid little attention to the food, however. It was the people that interested me. Using the medicine man as a translator, I spoke to his mother.

"Are you happy here?"

She said that she was happy.

"What do you do?"

She said she made piki, baskets and pottery, and helped with gardening and building, in addition to her religious duties, which I would not understand. Her wrinkled brown prune of a face was smiling good-naturedly at me as she spoke.

"And that's all?"

She said that was enough.

"And you don't feel . . . trapped? Don't feel like a mere servant?"

She laughed, then she said I did not understand her way of life. She said she was the boss, like all Hopi women. It was she who owned the home. Her husband was only a guest there. The children would take their name from their mother, not their father. In fact, all the food in the house belonged, not to her husband, but to her. How then could she feel like a servant?

The medicine man went on translating, smiling broadly, "Mama says that among our people it is the woman who does all the worrying, but that's all right because she is the stronger sex."

I was appalled.

And now she was leaning forward, placing her wrinkled claw on my knee, speaking to me earnestly in her own language. Her adopted son was hard put to translate her rapid speech.

"She asks if you are happy," he said.

"Well...."

"She says she sees in your face you are not."

"I might as well admit it then," I said gloomily.

"She says she will give you the Hopi secret of happiness and long life."

A sudden stupid surge of hope overcame me. "Yes? Yes?" I cried.

"She says, do what your wife tells you."

All three Indians were nodding at me seriously. I, however, was struck dumb by a surge of the Black Ecstasy, a surge of absolute despair, as if I'd peeped through the gates of the Garden of Eden to see the perfect life we lived before we became civilized, and had had the door slammed in my face.

The sun was setting beyond the Golden Gate as I pedaled home, hating myself, the white man that I was, dying slowly, like all my kind, of my poisonous sexual pride. I'd have to ask Doc during our next session if I could actually add years to my life by simply redefining one word in my vocabulary.

The word "man."

My mother-in-law intercepted me on my way to my bedroom.

"Let me smell your breath." Mrs. Whittle leaned forward, sniffing suspiciously, like a huge white rabbit.

I breathed in her face obligingly.

She frowned. "You think you're clever, covering up the smell somehow, but you don't fool me. Once a drunk, always a drunk!" She looked at me almost fondly, or at least with relief. To her, it was great if I'd stayed out all last night and the following day on a bender. That meant, to her, that I was My Old Self again. And now she favored me with a grotesque wink. "Everyone has some little weakness. An extra slice of cake now and then for me, and for you . . . come along in the front room and I'll fix you a bit of the hair off the dog that bit you."

She clutched my arm and dragged me toward our home bar. How easy it would be to say yes, to please and reassure her, to have "some little weakness" so she could have her own little weakness without guilt. How easy it would be to roll effortlessly down the tracks of habit, how easy to be, once again, the person they all knew, the person I was supposed to be. The Black Ecstasy hummed softly in my head, blurring my vision, numbing my will.

She stepped behind the bar. "It's gin you like, isn't it?"

When I did not reply, she set out a shot glass, produced an unlabeled bottle, and poured.

I became aware of someone else in the room.

It was Ruth, sitting on the couch so quietly, a book in her lap, that I had not noticed her. Ruth, the teenaged replica of Marge. Ruth, who might or might not be my daughter. (She did not resemble me in any way.) Ruth was pretending not to watch me, but I knew she could see my reflection out of the corner of her eye in the mirror behind the bar.

Ruth had seen me drink before.

Ruth had, in fact, seen me drunk many times.

Yet on this particular night the scales of decision were balanced so finely, so evenly, a hair could tip them one way or the other, and I suddenly knew that this time, at least, *I could not drink in front of Ruth.* As I realized this I felt a rush of gratitude toward the young girl, a rush of warmth. Ordinarily, to be honest, I did not like her.

"No thank you, Mrs. Whittle," I said apologetically.

"What?" Mrs. Whittle's round face turned red. "It's already poured. If you don't drink it, it'll only go to waste."

"No thank you," I repeated meekly.

Ruth was trying to be invisible, there on the couch.

"This is expensive stuff," said Mrs. Whittle, beginning to get angry. "I can't just pour it down the toilet."

"I'm sorry."

She pushed the glass toward me. "Don't get on your high horse now, damn it!" She was angry, yes, but in her voice there was also a note of panic. I felt sorry for her, but not sorry enough to pick up the glass.

"Where's Marge?" I asked, trying to change the subject.

"Where do you think?"

Then Beggars Could Ride

"At the church?"

"Of course! The people in the musical depend on her. She wouldn't let them down just to sit around and wait for a husband who never comes home. She's a responsible person."

"Thank you, Mrs. Whittle."

I left her with her shot glass, knowing she wouldn't pour the gin down the toilet. It would be waiting for me when I returned. I wondered if I would have the guts to pour it down the toilet myself.

IT was only a rehearsal, and these rehearsals generally went on at least once a week for months, but Marge sang beautifully, with terrific expression. The musical was Cole Porter's *Wake Up and Dream* and the song was "I Loved Him but He Didn't Love Me." I could easily have burst into tears at the sweet irony and bitterness she put into it, but instead, at the end, I gave her a wild standing ovation, though some people onstage stared at me, annoyed, and she looked embarrassed. (There was nobody but me in the audience.)

The curtain came down and I went backstage.

Marge was chatting in a low voice with some other members of the cast, among whom I recognized the muscular, somewhat balding fellow I'd seen her kissing in the alley.

"You were the cat's meow, Marge," I told her as I approached the group. (She had genuinely impressed me.)

"So you came back," she said to me, with surprising emotion, so that it seemed to me she must care about me, must have been worried about me . . . it almost seemed the glimpse I'd caught of her with the big guy had been an optical illusion. But was that shifty look in his eye when he realized who I was an optical illusion?

Marge did not introduce me to him, or to any of her friends, though some of the women, probably because they knew about Marge's affair, peered at me pityingly from behind their masklike stage makeup.

Marge led me away to a far corner of the backstage area, and when we were reasonably safe from eavesdroppers, she said, "I want you to know I'm not angry. I can understand what a strain you've been under, laid off from your job, trying to stay on the wagon. So you broke down and went on a toot. Right?"

"Wrong!" I was annoyed by her words, but at the same

time puzzled and somewhat moved by the concern in her voice.

She grasped me by the wrist. "You don't have to keep up a front with me. I'm Marge. I'm not only your wife, I'm your partner, your pal. You can talk to me. No secrets between us. Right?"

The big guy was watching us from the other end of the backstage area, at the same time pretending to be deep in conversation with his friends.

When I didn't say anything, Marge went on, "I even understand that you might be thinking of scramming, running out on me, leaving me to take care of the family alone. That dumb doctor you're going to, he's pushing you into it. But you'd be making a mistake, Honey, a big mistake. Running away won't solve anything, because your problem is you, and you'll take you along no matter how far you run."

I said, "I liked the way you sang that song. You're good, Marge. I never realized you were so good."

"I've been improving," she said, flattered. "If you'd ever come down to the rehearsals, you'd have noticed. You should come down. Get involved. Come out of your shell and mix with people, instead of going to that creepy old doctor and riding around alone on your bike all the time. You could make friends here in the church, like I have."

Her big friend was still watching us.

I said, "I've never been much of a mixer."

"But that's your problem. Don't you see? No man is an island. You've got to join the human race, not be so standoffish. The first step is for you and me to have a talk, a real heart-to-heart talk."

I glanced around. "Here?"

"No, Silly. Listen, I'm done for the night. I'll go to the dressing room and change out of my costume; then you can walk me home. We'll talk, Honey. We'll really talk. You wait for me. Right?"

"Right."

"Don't run off."

"I won't."

"Promise?"

"I promise."

She hurried away, glancing back at me over her shoulder now and then as if afraid I might vanish.

When she was out of sight, I strolled over to the big guy. The people he was talking to edged away but he

Then Beggars Could Ride

hesitated, and I had him, back to the wall. "Hi," I said. "I'm Newton, Marge's husband."

"Pleased t'meetcha." He shook my hand with a sweaty palm. "I'm Leonard Patroni. Call me Lenny. I'm Marge's boss at the old sweat shop."

"I know about you and Marge."

"Yeah?"

"Yeah, and I mean *all* about you."

There was an awkward pause, then he said defiantly, "So you wanna make somethin' out of it, Buster?"

Up until that moment I had been more or less bluffing. Up until that moment there was the possibility I had misunderstood something that was actually perfectly innocent, but now I really did know. I felt like weeping, but I didn't. Instead I said, "Relax. It's okay. Only natural."

"Natural?" he said with suspicion.

"She's a normal woman. She needs something, something I can't give her."

"Yeah? What?"

"Didn't she tell you about me? About my little problem?"

"You mean the booze?"

"Not exactly. I'm impotent, you see." (This was a lie.)

"No kidding." He was relaxing now, almost sympathetic.

"Booze does that," I explained.

"Hey, dat's too bad, Pal." He gave me an awkward pat on the shoulder.

"Actually I'm glad she has someone like you, someone strong . . ." He smiled, pleased. ". . . someone she can fall back on if something happens to me."

"Hey, don't talk like that," he said with alarm. "Nothin' ain't gonna happen to ya."

"But if something does, you'll take care of Marge, won't you?"

He hesitated.

I demanded, "You aren't married, are you?"

"Me? Naw, not me!"

"You love her, don't you? You're not just stringing her along?"

"Hey, I ain't like dat! Ask anybody."

"Then you *will* watch out for her?"

"Well, I. . . . Sure. Sure I will."

"You're okay, Lenny." I shook his hand vigorously.

"Yer a pretty swell guy yerself," he said, grinning with sudden camaraderie.

As I walked away from him I felt like throwing myself at his feet and sobbing, "Please, please, leave her alone." I felt like it, but I didn't do it.

UNDER the moon and stars Marge and I strolled along a quiet tree-lined street in Chaplin. In my left hand I held her right hand; in my right hand I held the left handlebar of my bike. I had always regarded Marge as basically a hardcore fool, but now she was changing before my very eyes, werewolflike, into a philosopher. The metamorphosis was confusing and disturbing, but I thought, *It's Lenny. He's bringing out a different side of her.* Since he was, as far as I could tell, genuinely stupid, she could control him better by becoming wise, whereas I was a sucker for dumb blondes, or I had been until recently.

"You could be happy, Newton," she said, in her new philosopher voice.

"How?" At that moment I felt many emotions, none of which was happiness.

"You could accept yourself as you are, stop trying to be someone else. You're not such a bad guy. Certainly you've never done anything to deserve the death penalty. I mean, I accept you. Why can't you accept yourself?"

"I know me better than you do."

"I know you, Sweetie. Don't you think I know you? So you take a few drinks now and then. I don't always act like I should, either."

I thought, *You can say that again.*

I said, "I'm on the wagon."

She said, "You don't have to be. If it makes you happy to drink, you should do it. Whatever makes you happy, do it. I *want* you to be happy, Baby. When you suffer, I suffer. When you go to that damn doctor and come home brooding, when you ride around alone on your bike day after day, that's almost more than I can take."

"I like riding my bike. That's what makes me happy."

"Who are you trying to kid? You're just escaping!"

"It makes me happy to escape."

"Is that going to be your career from now on? Escaping? Riding your lousy bicycle all over the place? That's not a life, Honey! You can't do that forever."

I thought of Doc's veiled threats. "You're right about that, anyway."

"Of course I am. Listen, Hon, I could introduce you to my friends. They won't mind if you drink a little. Some of them—they drink so much they make you look like Carry Nation. You could have a little fun, have a few laughs. They'd love you, Newton. You know, when you're tipsy you're a very funny man."

I had a picture in my mind of a tiny room, so full of cigarette smoke you couldn't breathe, jammed full of drunks, elbow-to-elbow, wall-to-wall. Lenny and Marge were there, and some fat lady from the circus was French-kissing me while, from the bathroom, came the smell of vomit. Thinking about it, I felt kind of ill myself. The title of this picture—and I think everyone Marge knew but me would agree—was "Fun!"

"A bunch of lushes," I muttered.

"How can you, of all people, say that? They're respectable people, members of the church, pillars of the community, doctors, lawyers, businessmen! Did you know some of them own their own businesses?"

I thought, *She must mean Lenny*.

I said, "And stuffed shirts, too!"

"You stuck-up moron!" she snatched her hand away from me. "Who the hell do you think you—"

I broke in, "If you thought this was going to be the last thing you ever said to me, would you still talk like that?"

She was instantly subdued, but she said, with gentle bitterness, "You're going to do it to me, aren't you?"

"Do what?"

"Finally really kill yourself and stick me with the guilt."

She was wrong, but I couldn't tell her my true plans. She might find some way to stop me.

At our front door, while Marge was fumbling in her purse for her keys, Mr. Whittle let us in, though it was long past his usual bedtime. From the way he looked at me, I got the impression he wanted to talk to me. He soon got his chance.

For a few moments, while Marge was in the bathroom, he and I were alone together in the dim hallway. He glanced around apprehensively, then leaned toward me and whispered, "Listen, young fellow, if you're planning on getting out, do it soon, or they'll trap you like they trapped me."

Marge returned in a filmy white silk nightgown and said, "Will you stay with me tonight, Newton?"

I knew the old man was right, but I followed her into her bedroom anyway.

CHAPTER 5

"You won't be coming to see me much longer," said Doc, gazing at me moodily across his desk.

"Why not?" I said, surprised.

"You'll make your decision, and I'll be of no more use to you."

A gray, almost shadowless, light from the overcast sky outside his window illuminated his somber features.

"I'll still drop in now and then." I was apologetic.

"Stop that!" he said sharply. "I'm not playing guilt games with you. It's the simple truth. You'll come here to tell me your choice, I'll direct you to the proper cultural training agencies, and that will be that." He leaned forward. "But before we part, I feel I'd like you to understand me, to know the philosophy that makes me do what I do."

"Is this part of my therapy?"

"More a part of mine. You'll be the Doc for a change."

"Well, all right, but I think I know your philosophy already. It's decision that matters with you, first, last and always."

"Not decision alone," he corrected. "Decision and imagination."

"Imagination?"

"Yes, of course." His intense earnestness made me uncomfortable. "How can I explain? Let me give you an example. Did you know that at the World's Fair in Paris in 1878, a fellow named Mouchot exhibited a solar energy collector that drove a steam engine?"

"Really? That early?"

"If someone with an ounce of imagination had looked at that gadget, what would he have said? 'An interesting toy?' No, he'd have said, 'Here we have an energy source that will never run out, that has no theoretical limit. Here we have the technological base for a new and better society.' If he'd been a businessman, he'd have said, 'Here's a potential fortune for me, selling power which I get absolutely free.' If he'd been a statesman, he'd have said, 'Here's a potential cure for my nation's dependence on foreign fuel sources.' If he'd been a social reformer, he'd have said, 'Here's an end to coal mines, chimney sweeps and soot.' But nobody said these things. The Western World had already begun to develop technology based on fossil fuels—first coal, then petroleum—and they continued to drift along in this direction, though even then it was obvious that a day would come when there would be no more fossil fuel. They did not imagine. They did not decide. They drifted. Now that those resources, which we need for better things than fuel, are almost gone, the human race will suffer for their indecision forever.

Right up to the Year of the Great Cold there were actually people who *opposed* birth control! Again they did not imagine. They drifted, and eventually billions of people starved to death because of their indecision.

"What was the twentieth century? A tragic, disastrous mistake! A mistake that could have been avoided by the exercise of only a little imagination, only a little decision! It's incredible but true that the people of the twentieth century poured fortunes into the development of nuclear energy, which depended on uranium, a natural resource they would certainly use up in a matter of decades. And it was obvious from the beginning that waste products would be produced that would continue to be dangerous for centuries. Or are those examples too grandiose for you? Try this! It's incredible, but it's true, that manufacturers in that century used plastics and aluminum, materials remarkable for durability, to make products designed to be *thrown away*! In matters large and small the twentieth century was such a catastrophic error that, in a sense, the twenty-first century can be understood as an elaborate attempt to avoid making that error again, an attempt to go back to before the twentieth century and start over, this time using at least a tiny bit of imagination. Do you understand what I'm saying?"

I had been overwhelmed by the vehemence of his tirade, but actually did not see what he was driving at. I murmured, "Well—"

"That's what we techs are all about. Our first duty, above all else, is to *imagine*!"

"And the second duty . . . is to control," I said softly.

He paused, eyeing me thoughtfully, then said, "You were shocked the other day, weren't you, when you learned that I had the power, in some circumstances, to condemn people to death. You didn't like that."

"No, I didn't, Doc."

"If it gives you any comfort, I've never used that power. At least not yet. But it's no more power than is held by any king or president or even general. Any leader faces situations where he must send men, often innocent men, to their deaths. More, any leader must face the fact that, being human, he'll make mistakes and sooner or later kill some people for nothing."

I said uneasily, "I wouldn't want to be in the position of deciding other people's lives and deaths."

He looked at me steadily, seriously. "You won't be. At least not until you learn one unpleasant truth: He who will not kill, can not rule."

I did not pay much attention to the rest of what he said, except that I remember it was something about how people don't pay attention.

IN the Mormon community the man was boss; in the Hopi community the woman was boss. Oddly enough, of all the enclaves I'd visited (and by now I'd visited over twenty), only these two attracted me, especially the Mormon community, though it was the Hopi community that excited most strongly my erotic fantasy.

To be owned by a woman, totally and completely owned . . . as a fantasy it had a hypnotic, serpentine, luxurious fascination, but would the reality be equally luxurious, or simply unpleasant?

The Mormon community, on the other hand, seemed to offer all the sexual delights of the harem, plus an airtight, utterly respectable rationalization for them.

I read *The Book of Mormon* from cover to cover.

I asked myself if I could believe in it.

And that, of course, was a problem, because with the best will in the world, I couldn't bring myself to believe a single word of it.

I wondered if the Hopi Indian religion was as hard to swallow and, after reading up on it at the public library, concluded that it was, if anything, even harder.

I mean, can you really make it rain by dancing and singing? Really?

It began to look as if the price of admission to any society might be the surrender of sanity, that every one of them rested on a foundation of pure dream-dust. If this were so it might be, as Marge sometimes put it, futile to seek anything more than what I could find in "my own backyard." It might be the highest wisdom to take out a life membership in the friendly neighborhood delusion and "be myself" happily ever after.

Such thoughts never failed to bring on the mog, soft and gray on my brain, whispering that it was too bad I hadn't succeeded in killing myself, that I needed a drink, that every part of the universe was equally meaningless and stupid.

But in spite of everything, I at last stood in the center of the park in the center of Chaplin one sunny noon . . . and decided. The mog retreated, growling.

EVERYONE should have been asleep at three a.m.
It was then that I quietly packed my bag and tiptoed down the hall.
Everyone should have been asleep, but everyone wasn't.
"Hello, Dad," said Ruth.
I was speechless.
She was wearing a red bathrobe over her red Chinese pajamas, though in the dim light the reds were no more than different shades of gray. She leaned against her doorjamb, and I couldn't make out her face. In the odd light her face seemed black.
She said, in a sad ironic tone, "Are you going to ask me what I'm doing here?"
I stammered softly, "Y-yes, I mean—"
"I wanted to see you off." She stood clear of the doorjamb. "Come into the front room. We don't want to wake Mama, do we?"
She led the way.
When we were seated side by side on the couch, she said, "Mind if I smoke?"
I was momentarily outraged. I never knew she smoked. She was too young for that! But I said nothing and she lit up, using Marge's stainless-steel lighter. The flame briefly illuminated her serious doll-like, child-face, then there was only the moving point of red light that indicated the tip of her burning cigarette, and the black oval of her head weakly silhouetted against the gray window. In answer to a question I had not voiced, she said, "No, Mama doesn't know I'm on the weed, and you . . . you won't tell, will you?"
"No." My voice sounded tense, choked.
"You and I. We don't tell everything we do or think, do we?"
"I suppose not." Our voices were barely a murmur, but there was a chance that Marge might hear us. I broke into a cold sweat.
"Do you wonder how I knew you were leaving tonight?" The tip of her cigarette glowed more brightly for an in-

stant, then, as it dulled, a fog of smoke appeared around her head.

"Yes."

"You looked happy this afternoon. That's how I knew. The others don't know. They never know anything. They never see anything."

There was a long silence, then I blurted, "I want you to know I'm sorry—"

"Don't lie." There was a touch of contempt in her voice. "You're not sorry at all. Don't lie, like everybody else."

"I mean, I'm sorry we couldn't have talked more, gotten to know each other."

"Maybe if I'd been a boy—"

"No, that's not it."

"Oh, I see. It's because I don't look like you. You think I might not be your daughter, what with the way Mama sleeps around and all. That's it, isn't it?"

I said miserably, "I guess so." But it wasn't.

She said wistfully, "There's no way to know for sure, is there? But I am like you. Not on the outside. On the inside." She let that sink in. She was right. I knew it deep down. She was right. She had Marge's body, but it was my consciousness that by some miracle looked out at the world through her flapper-child eyes. Because Ruth never talked much, this was a fact I'd always completely overlooked. Until now.

I asked her, "You don't want me to go, do you?"

There was a long pause. She took another drag on her cigarette, inhaling deeply like the experienced smoker she was. She exhaled, then said softly, "What do you care?"

"You want me to stay?"

"Yes."

"Then I'll stay."

"You're lying again."

"No, I'm not. You smoke. Do you drink, too?"

"Yes."

"Let's drink to my change of heart. Okay?"

She did not answer.

I said, "What do you like?"

"Whiskey on the rocks."

"On the rocks, eh?" I got up and groped my way over to the bar. There was no ice in the ice bucket. I thought, *There's ice in the kitchen, in the freezing compartment of the refrigerator.* By touch I located the familiar shape of the whiskey bottle, gave it a shake to hear it slosh, to be

Then Beggars Could Ride

sure there was something in it, then took it with me as I felt my way slowly toward the kitchen.

I opened the refrigerator.

The light inside temporarily blinded me.

I heard the springs in the couch creak softly, back in the front room, as I stood there blinking. Was Ruth getting up, coming out to join me in the kitchen? No. They creaked again. She was just getting comfortable.

I opened the freezing compartment. There were the ice cubes, glistening in their trays. I touched one of the trays. I realized without surprise that I was very, very thirsty. But I stood motionless, right hand on the icetray, left hand clutching the whiskey bottle.

It would be so easy.

But so final.

I set the bottle on the drain board.

I carefully, silently closed the refrigerator.

I stepped to the back door, silently unlocked it, opened it.

"Dad?" Ruth called softly, anxiously, from the other room.

I sprang through the doorway onto the back porch, leaped down the steps, almost fell over my bike before I found it.

As I pedaled frantically away there was one point, where I turned from the backyard onto the alley, where I could look back for a second and see a figure in bathrobe and pajamas standing in the starlight on the back porch, watching me.

Ruth did not shout after me or raise an alarm.

But she didn't wave goodbye either.

A DAY had passed and most of a night.

Above and slightly ahead of me, half-hidden by a light fog and the pre-dawn semi-darkness, the triple-decked Golden Gate Bridge murmured with traffic. Leaning on a gunwale and tilting back my head, I could dimly glimpse an electric freight train moving swiftly along the lowest deck, a few electric trucks with yellow-haloed headlights passing on the middle deck, and on the top deck, almost lost from view, a handful of early-bird bicyclists. It seemed curiously significant, for some reason, that the bicyclists were on the top deck, that wherever there were multi-level transportation arteries, the bicyclists and pedestrians were on top.

I had never seen the Golden Gate Bridge from below before, or from so close a range. I wondered if, after today, I would ever see it again, even from a distance.

I was standing on the damp slippery deck of the clipper ship, *The Flying Dutchman,* with nothing to do for the time being, but stare. The ship was in a lock at the north end of the tidal dam that blocked the mouth of San Francisco Bay, a dam that produced electric power for local high-energy functions such as the railroad and the clusters of high-energy factories on the nearby shores. The muffled hum of dynamos was exciting, almost sinister, to someone who had been born and raised in an environment of low-energy technology.

The water level in the lock seemed to be going down much too slowly, though I suppose it must have been emptying at a normal rate. It was as if the *Dutchman* were a prisoner, and I was impatiently awaiting its release.

Captain Marlinspike joined me at the rail. "It's a cold morning, sailor. Better put on a jacket," he advised me. He himself had his navy blue peacoat well buttoned up, and there was indeed a light but cold breeze from behind us.

I answered, "I don't have a jacket, sir."

"Get a sweater out of your luggage then."

"I don't have any luggage, sir."

He eyed me shrewdly through his steel-rim spectacles. "You had to make a quick getaway, eh?"

"You might say so, sir. I got out with the clothes on my back and my bike. Everything else I had to leave behind."

"Hmm. This your first time at sea?"

"Yes, sir."

"What did you say your name was?"

"McClintok, sir."

"You're about my size, Mr. McClintok. I've an old peacoat that should fit you. I'll send the cabin boy for it."

"Why, thank you, sir!"

"Don't thank me, Mr. McClintok. That jacket's coming out of your pay." He studied me for a moment before adding, "I can't expect an honest answer to this, but are you running away from the techs?"

An image of Doc flashed through my mind. I hadn't told Doc my decision, gone through the "cultural training" he'd mentioned, or even informed him of my departure. He probably wouldn't know I'd gone anywhere until I failed to turn up for my weekly session four days from now. I said (was it a lie?), "Not the techs, sir. My wife."

He chuckled. "Half the crew could say the same, but mark you," he was serious again, "it wouldn't be wise to try to dodge the techs. No, not wise at all. They've ways of finding a man, and if you get on the wrong side of 'um, they can be more than somewhat unpleasant." He shook his head ruefully.

There was a yell from the foredeck.

Hearing it, the captain brightened. "The sea gates are opening, Mr. McClintok," he said with suppressed excitement. "You fall to with the rest of the crew and do as they do. Understand?"

"Aye, sir." I had a feeling the sailor-talk sounded odd, coming from me.

As the gates at the mouth of the lock opened, the waves from the sea entered, and the *Dutchman* began to rock gently, her three tall masts swaying, her rigging swinging. The sailors, without waiting for a command, had been scrambling into position, and now Cap Marlinspike shouted, "Pick up those towlines, lads! Shantyman, give us a tune!"

"Ready now?" came a light tenor voice from the foredeck.

There were two ropes, knotted at intervals, lying on the deck, one on the port side and one to starboard. They ran the length of the ship. Far aft, they turned around a pair of barrel-sized wheels, from which they continued on to the two sides of the lock, being finally secured to heavy posts on either side of the mouth of the lock.

The crew, including myself, faced aft and picked up the ropes.

The fine clear tenor voice of the shantyman sang out in a heavy measured rhythm, so loud it startled into flight several gulls who'd been perched on a yardarm, "Ol' Boney was a warrior!"

His solo voice was answered by the chorus of the full crew, "Away, ay-yah!" On the "yah" we all pulled as one man on the ropes. The ship moved forward very slightly. I thought, *They're actually singing! What a mim!*

As the shantyman sang again, we rested, then took another grip on the lines. "A warrior and a terrior!" he sang.

"John Franswah!" we sang in reply, pulling on the "wah."

On the second pull the forward motion of the ship was

more pronounced, and as we rested the ship continued to move forward.

The shantyman sang a third time, "Boney beat the Prooshians!"

And the crew sang, "Away, ay-yah!"

The prow passed beyond the gates and the rolling of the ship increased. An old man in a yellow raincoat and rainhat was walking on one edge of the lock, keeping pace with us. A younger man walked on the other edge. The old man waved his lantern and called in a wheezing voice, "Give me love to the Panama girls!"

The shantyman sang, "Boney beat the Rooshians!"

We all sang, "John Franswah!" and pulled.

It wasn't easy pulling that knotted rope, but it gave me an odd satisfaction. I thought of the science fiction writers of the nineteen-twenties who'd predicted a world where machines did all the work, even the thinking. They'd been dead wrong. There was still a place for human muscle and brain, and I was glad of it.

"Boney went to Elba!"

"Away, ay-yah!"

The outer face of the dam came into view, streams of white water pouring from it. The men in the raincoats stopped walking and fell behind us. They stood next to the snubbing posts on either side of the gates, watching us go. I could no longer see the old man clearly, only his lantern.

"Boney he come back!"

"John Franswah!"

We were clear of the lock.

"Hold there, shantyman!" the captain commanded, and the singing ceased. "Free the towlines!" he called.

Behind us I heard two splashes as the nooses of the towlines, freed from the snubbing posts, hit the water. From the distance came the cry, "Lines free." The ship continued to coast.

The crew had dropped the towlines and were now taking new positions—all but me. I didn't know what my new position was.

"Ready for sail?" shouted Cap Marlinspike.

"Aye," the crew responded in chorus.

The captain's voice was exultant. "Now!"

The sails on all three masts unfurled simultaneously with a rush and a thump. The breeze had not seemed

Then Beggars Could Ride

strong, but it filled the sails, billowing them out. The ship heeled over sharply, partly righted itself, and began to gain speed.

I was near enough to the captain to see his eyes glittering with delight and to hear him whisper to himself, "Beautiful!"

He went quickly aft with a crouching, catlike gait and took the wheel.

The mist was thinning, the wind rising. Far off to my right I saw the Point Bonita light, the hills dark behind it. The sky brightened rapidly, silhouetting a flock of screeching seagulls that wheeled above the ship's wake. In moments the sun would appear.

And I?

I stood at the rail, facing the dark uncreated void ahead, the void that was my freedom.

I chuckled with delighted fear.

PART TWO

CHAPTER 6

The layover in Monterey Bay had been brief, but I'd had a chance to visit, together with a few other crew members, the remarkable community of Carmel. Carmel had not waited for the Year of the Great Cold to say no to progress, but had reached its final form somewhere in the middle of the twentieth century. After that it resisted even such seemingly harmless new-fangled inventions as sidewalks and street numbers.

I met, but did not really get to know, the Abalone Eaters Club, a small group of devoted anachronists whose lives were given up to recreating the lives of a certain specific group of artists and writers in the year 1907.

I learned their song, which goes like this:

> "Oh, some folks boast of quail on toast
> Because they think it's toney,
> But I'm content to owe my rent
> And live on abalone."

There's more, but I can't remember it.

One of the club took the role of Jack London, another the role of George Sterling, another his wife Carrie. There was one who had made himself a mim of Clark Ashton Smith, another was Ambrose Bierce, and there was a Jimmy Hopper, a Xavier Martinez, a Porter Garnett . . . at least seventy people in all who had totally taken on the personae of Jack London's literary coterie and were now acting out, one day at a time, a year in their lives.

I knew something about them from high school literature courses, and one thing that I knew was that the beautiful poetess, Nora May French, had committed suicide by taking cyanide in the very year they were acting out. I took the young lady who was playing Nora May French to one side at the picnic where I met her and tried to warn her.

"In a few months the real Nora May French poisoned herself," I said.

"I know," she answered.

"Are you going to do the same?"

"Of course." She had a wistful, fatalistic smile.

"You can't!"

I'll never forget her answer. "Don't worry. Next year,

when we do 1907 again, someone else will be recruited to replace me."

There was, it seems, actually a waiting list of women who wanted to act her part, suicide and all.

But now we were at sea again, southbound in sight of the California coast, on a clear, warm, sunny afternoon. The *Dutchman* was carrying plenty of sail—even the studding sails were set outside the square sails on booms rigged out through rings on the yardarms—and we were plowing into the swells with a regular thump, splash, swish, thump, splash, swish.

Cap Marlinspike had been giving me a few lessons in seamanship and instructing me in my own duties on the *Dutchman*, but the conversation had lagged. For lack of anything better to say, I began to tell him about Nora May French, finishing with, "I can't understand someone like that."

"I can," said the Captain.

"To give one's life as part of an act? You can understand that?"

"Indeed I can, Mr. McClintok. We all do the same. Back when there was wars, soldiers would almost always think of the role they were playing first and their lives second. Ain't that right?"

"Well . . . I suppose so, sir."

"And sailors, eh? It's more important to a real sailor whether the sails are taken down in a storm than that his life might be in danger. Mark what I say, Mr. McClintok, it's not a man's life that matters, but the role he plays, and to die well. Ah, that's the ambition of every one of us. To die well, that's better than all the gold and fame and lovin' ladies the world has to offer. To actually be Nora what's-her-name is nothing much. I wager she killed herself over some worthless dandy. That's usually the way of it. But this one that kills herself as part of a mim of Nora . . . that's what I call a real trooper. The show must go on! All the world's a stage! Y'see what I mean? Show business! I understand in the nineteen-twenties, when they made those super-spectacular movies, a few stuntmen and stagehands always got killed. And what about auto races, eh? And in the Middle Ages, what about tournaments? And in Ancient Rome, what about gladiatorial games? I've seen enough men die, when the sea got frisky, so it don't mean a thing to me no more, but a man who can play the role he's chosen, come what may . . . that man can still impress me."

"Even if it means death, sir?" I said gloomily.

"Especially if it means death!" He gave me a hearty slap on the back.

It was at that moment I first noticed the black clouds on the horizon.

IT had become painfully obvious we would not reach Morro Bay before the storm hit, and there was nothing else within range that could be called a safe harbor. Rather than risk running aground, the *Dutchman* swung farther out to sea as the wind rose and the waves grew taller.

I was working on the afterdeck with the shantyman, who'd been given the job of continuing my nautical education, when I overheard the captain say to the first mate, "Barometer's falling fast. I've been radioing the weather boys on shore, and they're as surprised as we are. This storm wasn't due for at least a day."

The mate, who'd taken the wheel, answered soberly, "The weather's turning freakish, like it was in the decade before the Year of the Great Cold. You suppose the Cold is comin' back?"

"If it is, the world is ready for it this time," said the captain.

A twenty-four-oar, Phoenician bireme, not much larger than one of our longboats, passed us heading in the opposite direction. It was a shallow-draft vessel and light enough so the crew, if they got safely to a beach, could pick it up and carry it inland out of harm's way.

In grim earnest our own crew set to work preparing for the blow, putting storm gaskets on the furled topsails, lowering and stowing the foresail and spanker and taking in the two inner jibs. In the one remaining jib we put a single reef, and a single reef in the mainsail.

The storm hit us full force a half hour after sundown. The first great rush of rain and wind almost capsized the ship, but she righted quickly, and Marlinspike sheered her bow to within five points of the wind. At his shouted command the crew leaped into action, except for me. I still had so little knowledge of the seaman's craft that I was worse than useless, so I stood on the afterdeck near the wheel and hung on. I can tell you now what they were doing, but at the time it was all a mystery, and all their

Then Beggars Could Ride

commands jibberish. I quickly understood that it was vital to hold the wind behind us, not to take it from the side, for fear of foundering, but beyond that I knew nothing.

The mate was shouting, his voice almost lost in the howling gale, "Too much canvas!"

"Two more reefs in the mainsail!" commanded the captain.

To make reefs, we had to lower the mainsail, and to do this, we would have to fall off before the wind. But it must be done.

It was so dark I could not see anyone, not even the captain who stood nearby at the wheel, and I could only dimly hear the shouts of the seamen ahead and above me as they struggled with the sails. And now, abruptly, the *Dutchman's* bow swung off of its own accord. The mainsail must be down!

The captain was swearing as he wrestled the wheel, and with a kind of sick horror I felt the wind swing from behind me to my left side. In a moment we would take the full force of the storm broadside, and there was nothing anyone could do to prevent it. I gripped the nearest stays and braced myself as best I could.

For a moment we were dropping, then, with a jolt, we began to rise, and the fury of the storm calmed as we entered the wind-shadow of the wave we were climbing. Dimly I saw the top of the wave above me, a dull-white writhing blur.

The impact almost pulled me free, but I clung on to the stays somehow as I found myself under water, the sea forcing itself up my nostrils, down my throat, drowning me, suffocating me, pulling my feet out from under me.

An instant later I was above water again, coughing and sputtering and gasping for air, but still clinging to the stays. Nearby I heard a curious whirring sound. It was a moment before I recognized what it was. The wheel! It was spinning freely. The captain was gone and there was nobody at the wheel!

I then recalled that there was nobody but me near the wheel, nobody but me to grab the wheel and turn the ship before the next big wave or the one after it rolled the *Dutchman* bottomside up!

I had a sense of the rhythm of the waves, knew how long I had until the next wave hit. The ship was going down now, and in an instant we'd be rising to meet the next crest. I had just enough time.

I abandoned the relative safety of my grip on the stays and launched myself across the steeply slanting deck toward the whirring noise.

The spokes of the wheel were spinning like an airplane propeller; they almost broke my fingers before I could drag them to a stop. Another wave went over me, almost carrying me away, but I hung on and, when I surfaced, immediately began turning the wheel in the opposite direction. I was actually surprised when the ship responded. It came about sluggishly, but it came about.

I was steering the ship!

I couldn't believe it.

But now we were no longer broadside to the storm. It was behind me, hurling rain at my back each time I came up out of the wind-shadow. I laughed out loud with sheer exhilaration.

A man came lunging across the deck and slammed into me. "Who's that?" he demanded. It was Cap Marlinspike.

"McClintok, sir," I answered.

He took the wheel, wheezing and coughing. "That wave almost got me, lad!" he gasped. "I was down in the scuppers with the wind knocked outta me. Damn near went overboard! But you stepped in and saved us all, you did. You're not a sailor yet, but you've got a sailor's guts. I vow, sir, as long as I'm captain there'll always be a berth on the *Dutchman* for you!"

"Thank you, sir." Trying to salute him on the heaving deck, I lost my balance and fell, almost sliding into the scuppers myself.

His attention was no longer on me. As I picked myself up I heard him shout, "Cut loose the jib halyard and sheet!"

"Aye, sir," came the strangled voices of the crew out of the darkness, and in a moment we were running under bare poles. It was, as it turned out, an unnecessary precaution. The worst of the storm had passed.

CHAPTER 7

It was early morning in Los Angeles. The air was clear and fresh, without a trace of the smog and pollution that, according to Cap Marlinspike, had once made the city all but unlivable, before either of us was born. I sat on the rail in the worn but serviceable peacoat the captain had given me. (He changed his mind about taking it out of my pay.) He'd given me a duffel bag too, in fact a whole sailor's outfit. My few minutes at the wheel of the *Dutchman* had impressed him more, I thought, than it was really worth.

Beyond the rail was the dock, and beyond the dock the warehouses, and beyond the warehouses the buildings of an enclave that looked oddly familiar. When the captain stopped at my side, I questioned him about it.

"That's Sherlock," he told me.

"Sherlock?"

"A mim of London, Victorian London, not so much as it actually was, but the way it was in the Sherlock Holmes stories. Perhaps you've heard the Vincent Starrett quotation: 'There can be no grave for Sherlock Holmes or Watson. Shall they not always live in Baker Street? Are they not there this instant as one writes? Outside the hansoms rattle through the rain, and Moriarty plans his latest devilry. Within, the sea-coals flame upon the hearth, and Holmes and Watson take their well-won ease. So they still live for all that love them well: in a romantic chamber of the heart: in a nostalgic country of the mind: where it is always 1895.' Well, this is it."

"London in Los Angeles?"

"Not such an odd combination, Mr. McClintok. They both have the fog, y'know."

"And in this London there is a Sherlock Holmes and a Dr. Watson?"

"At 221B Baker Street, yes."

"How much of London do they have here?"

"Only the central metropolitan area. Where Middlesex would be, there's a different enclave, and yet another one where you might expect to find Essex."

"It might be interesting to settle down here," I mused.

Marlinspike frowned. "I'd not be in a hurry to do that, if I were you."

"What makes you say that? Is it just because you want me to stay in your crew or—"

He broke in, "You're welcome to stay with the *Dutchman*, of course, but after the reception the sea gave you, I'd not blame you if you never set foot in a ship again. It's not that, Mr. McClintok. It's the people here. You remember that poetess?"

"You mean Nora May French?"

"Aye, that's the one. You thought she was playing the game a bit too serious, as I recall. Well, here in Los Angeles there's many that play it more serious yet. Up north you can enter and leave most enclaves pretty much as you like. Here it's not like that. Here people are all for keeping the enclaves pure, not dilutin' the mim. In the first place, it ain't easy getting in, and in the second place, once you're in it ain't easy getting out. And while you're in you gotta obey all the local laws, which can be very strange ones at times. These are the descendants of the actors and directors and technical crews of Old Hollywood, the greatest illusion-factory of all time, and they tend to play very heavy indeed."

"What do the techs think about these closed-door policies?"

"The techs don't like it, of course, but the techs are caught on the horns of a dilemma here, y'see. They're against restrictions on personal freedom, where these ain't essential, but on the other hand if they stepped in to force open the enclaves, it'd be said the techs themselves was restricting personal freedom. Meanwhile the locals get steadily more repressive. They've a single unified police force here. If you break a crazy law in one enclave it's no use fleeing to another. The coppers will follow you, just changing uniforms as they pass from one mim to another, and they'll nail you even if what you did is no crime in the mim where you're caught. Sooner or later the techs are goin' to put a stop to that, but in the meantime. . . ." He shrugged eloquently.

"All the same," I said, "I'd like to visit this enclave, and maybe one or two others. I'll be careful not to break any laws."

He looked at me broodingly for a while before speaking. "If you must you must, lad. But mark me well, though I like you, though I think you've the makings of a fine seaman, I'll not risk my own neck or the necks of any of

Then Beggars Could Ride

my crew comin' in to rescue you if you get in trouble."

"I didn't expect you to," I said, annoyed.

"And though, as I say, I like you, Mr. McClintok, this ship sails in one week from now, no later, and if you ain't aboard when she sails, that's too bad for you."

"One week, you say?"

"Aye. And we're goin' round the horn, you know. We won't be back this year, and maybe not next year either. What I mean to say is, goodbye is goodbye, Y'understand?"

"I understand."

"Well then, since I see you'll not listen to reason, at least let me give you directions. Before you can even walk the streets, you needs papers, and the papers you get at Scotland Yard. That's the New Scotland Yard, as they call it, corner of Whitehall and Downing Street. You go down the gangplank, turn right and follow the Thames Embankment. It's a huge place with round turrets at the corners, windows in the roof, and trees out front, right next to the river. You can't miss it. You go on in and take your place in the waitin' room."

"Who do I ask to see?"

He laughed. "Who would y'think, mate?"

"How should I know?"

"Inspector Lestrade, of course!"

IT wasn't as easy as Marlinspike made out to get from the West India docks, where the *Dutchman* was moored, to the offices of the Metropolitan Police at New Scotland Yard, even with my bicycle. Because of the obstruction of buildings that ran right to the water's edge, I was almost immediately forced to leave the Thames and wander through the maze of London streets, constantly at the risk of getting lost or getting arrested for not having papers. I had to stop passersby several times and ask directions. (Needless to say, I did not ask any officers of the law.)

I had to admire the authenticity of the mim. Sherlock followed the model of London in greater detail than I had hitherto dreamed possible. Even the smell, caused largely by the numerous horse-drawn vehicles, was perfectly in period. Most striking of all, however, was the condition of the people: so many were ragged, dirty and obviously unhappy. Other mims had contented themselves with reproducing only the good side of their particular periods in history. Even the slaves were happy—it was fun. Sherlock reproduced the bad as well. I understood, at last, what the element had been that was lacking in every other mim I'd visited, making them all seem false and unreal.

The missing element was oppression.

Perhaps, I thought, one could have a utopia or a good mim, but not both.

When dismounted I found myself solicited not only by street peddlers of every conceivable product, and beggars of both sexes and all ages, but by little barefoot doll-like prostitutes, girls who could not have been more than twelve or thirteen years old.

"Hey Gov'ner!" they'd call, "I can make a poor sailorman 'appy, I can!" or "Lookin' for a girl, sir?"

Along the same streets, in carriages, coaches and hansom cabs, rode gentlemen and ladies whose expressions were so prim and proper and clothing so stiff and orderly it seemed unlikely they could unbend enough to reproduce, yet often they had one or two equally prim children with them. I caught a glimpse of a newspaper: the headlines told of a man who'd been given the death penalty for seducing a girl of, as they put it, "good family." The death penalty!

"Hey there sailorman," called a little girl.

I mounted my bike and rode hastily on.

Yes, this city horrified me, I must admit, yet at the same time it fascinated me. There was immorality in other enclaves: Chaplin was proud of its freedom from old-fashioned morality. But here, though good and bad lived side by side, there *was* a good and bad. It wasn't a matter of "Everything Goes." There was an upright, decent way to live here, at least for those who could afford it, and even those not upright and decent themselves seemed to respect those who were. I watched the doffed caps, heard the respectful "sirs" and "m'ams." Tradition! Tradition meant something here. And I noticed how, when the men spoke, their women fell silent. That didn't happen in Chaplin. In Chaplin women had no respect for anything, least of all for their husbands.

The first horror quickly passed, and I realized I liked Sherlock, liked it better than any other mim I'd yet seen. It was, somehow, more real.

At Blackfriars Bridge I found the Victoria Embankment and was once again able to pedal along the shore of the

Then Beggars Could Ride

river, as it turned out, all the way to New Scotland Yard, passing under Waterloo Bridge and the Hungerford Railroad Bridge on the way.

There was an actual yard, of sorts, inside the high brick walls of the Scotland Yard building, and in that yard, where I found a number of bicycles already parked, I left my own. I entered the massive, forbidding building through an entrance marked "Alien Control."

At the end of a dim hallway I located a room where a crowd of sailors and other "aliens" stood in line before a dark-stained, wood counter. On the other side of the counter a staff of clerks worked busily. (I noted the office crew was entirely male.)

I bypassed the waiting line and went straight to the counter. "Can you help me, please?" I asked the nearest clerk, a skinny awkward fellow with an eyeshade and a surprisingly bright red vest from which hung his watch and chain.

He looked at me, surprised, then said, "Who do you wish to see?"

"Inspector Lestrade," I told him.

"Did he send for you?"

"No."

"Do you have an appointment?"

"Well . . . no."

"Then would you please go to the end of the line?" His voice carried a tone of lofty disdain.

I had no choice but to obey, and soon found myself standing behind the last man in the line, a small brown man, probably a Hindu judging from his turban and pajama-style pants and shirt.

A large pendulum clock with Roman numerals on its face hung on the wall beyond the counter, ticking with a slow, weary monotony. Except for the murmur of voices from the clerks, who all spoke as softly as if in a church, this clock was the only sound in the room. After I had been standing for some time, the clock solemnly tolled the hour of two. It was already two in the afternoon. I'd taken longer than I'd thought getting here.

A door opened in the back of the room and two men emerged. One was a bearded sea captain, the other, I realized from the respect everyone showed him, must be Lestrade.

Lestrade was a small, thin, ferretlike man, neat and

dapper after the fashion of the period, with his tailored gray suit, tapered trousers and plaid vest. He wore a high stiff collar—the detachable kind—and his dark hair was cut in neat sideburns, though he had neither beard nor mustache. It was his eyes that most caught my attention: dark, beady, glittering, disturbingly intelligent. If appearance meant anything, Lestrade (at least this Lestrade) was by no means the fool portrayed in the stories by Conan Doyle. I watched him shake hands with the sea captain, then thoughtfully draw a package of cigars from his inside suitcoat pocket, light one, and stand puffing on it as the captain sat down with the fellow with the red vest at a nearby desk.

The line moved forward slightly as another of those waiting to see Lestrade passed through a swinging half door in the counter and disappeared, along with the little detective, into the rear office.

The clock ticked on.

The captain left, some official-looking papers clutched in his hand.

I noticed that a handsome, clean-shaven gentleman with an expression of utter boredom was gazing down at us from a bronze-framed steel engraving high on the wall. According to the title-plate, this was a portrait of Sir Robert Peel, founder of the Metropolitan Police.

I whispered to the Hindu in front of me, "How long have you been waiting?"

"A day and a half, *sahib*." His voice was subdued and courteous and very, very patient.

From the head of the line came a Scottish burr, also patient, though bitter. "And I a week and a day."

A week and a day? I could spend the entire time the *Dutchman* was in port standing in this line!

I asked the Hindu, "But in the meantime, before you get your papers, where do you live?"

"In the Holy Land, *sahib*."

"The Holy Land?" I echoed incredulously.

A redheaded Irishman chimed in, amused. "Aye lad. The Holy Land's a slum, y'know, for the unwanted foreign element, if y'take my meaning. The coppers don't go in there much, as it ain't good for their health." There was a ripple of subdued laughter in the crowd.

The man in the red vest glanced over at us and frowned.

"You mean everyone who comes to Sherlock has to

Then Beggars Could Ride

stand in line for a week and live in a slum?" I demanded.

The Irishman answered, "A bit of a bribe might speed things up."

The Scotsman glumly contradicted him. "They don't take bribes here at the Yard, more's the pity. This treatment is naught but a subtle hint to us all. We're not wanted." There was a general murmur of assent.

The Irishman looked at me, arms akimbo, head cocked to one side. "Hey sailor, might you be thinkin' Scotland Yard was founded to fight crime?"

"Well, wasn't it?" I said.

"Faith no, lad! It's to keep out the Irish!"

The laughter this time was louder than before.

The man in the red vest came over to the counter and snapped, "No talking in the lines, there, gentlemen." There was more than a hint of sarcasm in the way he said "gentlemen."

It took me less than a minute to come to a decision. "To Hell with the papers," I muttered under my breath, then turned and strode out.

Outside under the bright open sky I breathed a sigh of relief, feeling myself once again a free man. Then I started looking for my bicycle.

It was gone.

The bikes remaining were all of an old-fashioned style, in-period for Sherlock and, I noticed for the first time, all locked. I had not locked mine, thinking it would be safe right in front of the police station, and anyway I'd been used to the Bay Area, where theft was almost unknown.

There was a uniformed policeman standing nearby, arms behind his back, staring vacantly into space. I went up to him and demanded, "Did you see someone take a bicycle that didn't belong to him?"

He asked reasonably enough, "How am I to tell the difference between a man taking his own bike and a man taking someone else's?"

I was about to protest when I focused on the officer's face. He was not friendly, not friendly at all. I was an alien, and the real purpose of Scotland Yard was, it seemed, to "control" aliens. He might be polite, this big "copper" who stood looming over me, but he wasn't intending to put himself out for me the least little bit. In fact, if I made a fuss, he might very well start asking me for my papers.

I swallowed my anger, tipped my sailor's cap to the policeman, and wandered aimlessly away.

Westminster Bridge was nearby. I walked out to the middle of it and stood, elbows on the rail, gazing down at the brown water. I thought of Marge. We'd had a lot of fun together, Marge and I. I thought of Ruth, who probably was my daughter after all. I thought of my bicycle.

They were gone now, all gone.

I thought of my name.

I wasn't Newton or McClintok to these strangers around me. I was "sailor." It was an identity I shared with anyone else who happened to be wearing a peacoat. I wasn't even "Jack" anymore. There was no home I could reach before nightfall, except perhaps the ship, and a ship is not a home. It's a vehicle, a way of getting to someplace that might be a home. A painful tension appeared in my chest. It wasn't the Black Ecstasy. It wasn't any kind of ecstasy. It was simple, uncomfortable, annoying pain.

Tears began to trickle down my cheeks. I was crying, but nobody cared. People walked past me, laughing and gossiping, paying no attention to me. What was I to them?

I could have jumped off the bridge.

I didn't.

Instead I began the long weary trudge back to the ship.

FEELING restless I awoke before dawn, and got dressed quietly, so as not to disturb my shipmates in the cramped narrow bunkroom, then I went up on deck.

A heavy fog lay over the West India Docks, but there was enough light for me to dimly see the forest of masts and rigging standing silently all around me. Except for a few haloed gaslights in the distance, I could not make out a trace of the Blackwall district on the port side, nor of the Isle of Dogs to starboard. On the foredeck two sailors stood watch. I could not see them but I could hear the murmur of their tired voices; they, of course, could not see me. This was just as well, because they could not have failed to notice I had my duffle bag with me; they could not have failed to ask me where I was going and if I planned ever to come back. To these questions I had no answers. I was not even certain that I would go ashore now, in the middle of the night. Had anyone spoken to me, tried to talk me out of it, he would have had an easy time of it. I had no rational reason for what I was doing, or at least nothing that would stand up to the least breath of argument.

Yet there was something about the orderliness, the tradition, the—it's not easy to say this—the morality of Sherlock that attracted me irresistibly. It was a place where Marge, with her messy liberalism, would never fit in, and therefore it might turn out to be exactly right for me. The fact that this society didn't welcome me, didn't seem to want "my kind," made it all the more attractive, like a party to which only the Right People are invited.

There were, I knew, places in the district called "The Holy Land" where I could hide out, where I could stay until I got the all-important Papers, where I could probably live as cheaply as it was possible to live in this mim of Victorian London. (I still had my sailor's pay for my brief voyage on the *Dutchman*, but it was not much. I'd have to stretch it.)

Well, what was I waiting for?

I tossed my duffle bag onto the dock. It made quite a loud thump, but the murmur of conversation from the men on watch continued undisturbed. They had probably taken the sound for the bump of a ship against the pier, or some such thing.

When I was sure that they were paying no attention, I clambered over the rail, found the heavy cable that secured the stern to the dock, and began climbing down it, hanging from my hands and legs. Would the men on watch have stopped me if I'd simply walked down the gangplank? Probably ... for my own good!

The cable, which had been taut, now began, under my weight, to slacken, drawing the afterdeck slowly toward the dock, lowering me toward the water. I'd forgotten how easy it is to set a ship in motion. For a moment I was afraid I was in for a dunking, but there wasn't much play in the ropes, and the forward hawser pulled tight and stopped the ship long before I got wet.

As I swung there, more or less upside down, it occurred to me that a few months ago I wouldn't have been able to do this. I wouldn't have had the strength. This thought gave me a rush of delight. I was indeed changing, turning into a new and better man. Simple health and physical strength, it seemed to me at that moment, were at least half the secret of happiness.

There was a metal disk, a sort of shield, on the cable. The shield was intended to block the passage of rats, but it nearly blocked my passage as well; I had a devil of a time getting past it, but I did.

When, at last, I had the firm timbers of the dock under my feet, I was pleased to note I was hardly sweating. This was a new body I had, a body that let me do things with ease I couldn't have done at all before. I picked up my duffle, touched my cap to the still-invisible men on watch who continued to converse in low, bored voices, and walked swiftly but silently away from the *Dutchman.*

There were policemen at the gate to the pier, but they kept to the light of the lantern that hung above the door of their guard hut. I kept to the darkness and, when their backs were turned, slipped easily past them.

I made sure I was well out of earshot before chuckling to myself and breaking into a trot down the damp, echoing, empty cobblestone street.

THE Covent Garden Market at four in the morning was as swarming with life as if it had been broad daylight. In the light of hundreds of lanterns, plus the gaslight streetlamps spaced at regular intervals around the rectangular marketplace, buyers, shopkeepers, hoteliers and pushcart vendors loudly conducted their business with the stolid wholesalers who had transported, largely by wagon, an incredible bounty of fruits, vegetables and flowers to this spot in the middle of Sherlock.

From where?, I wondered.

Sherlock was much larger than most enclaves, and did not follow the hexagonal pattern I was accustomed to. The farming area might be anywhere. And while most of the lanterns seemed to be burning vegetable oils, I could have sworn I smelled, now and then, the forbidden aroma of petroleum. One of the men I'd heard called "costers" elbowed past me in the crowd, dressed in a long velvet jacket, cord trousers gathered at the knees and elaborately stitched boots. His costume suggested clowning, the circus, but his expression was grim and crafty.

There were beggars here, and prostitutes (though fewer of the very young ones I'd seen near the docks), and once I glimpsed a pair of pickpockets at work. This criminal activity took place against the incongruous backdrop of the imposing Royal Opera House that overlooked the

Then Beggars Could Ride

square on one side like a dozing alderman, while the west side was filled by the low, solemn-porticoed St. Paul's Church.

More incongruous yet, this was the site of the Bow Street Police Station, which, as an old flower woman told me, was once the headquarters of the Bow Street Runners, the city's first police force. Uniformed officers came and went constantly, but none of them so much as glanced at the prostitutes, beggars and pickpockets. (The old women called the pickpockets "fingersmiths," with obvious admiration.)

When a knife-fight broke out—as it did shortly after I arrived—the police picked up the wounded loser in a "hand ambulance," little more than a three-wheeled pushcart, but otherwise took no action. They did not even question any of the multitude of witnesses.

I hated to see these things, but mainly, I admit, for a personal reason. What I saw was doing serious damage to my image of Sherlock as a bastion of order, tradition and respectability. The worst was a gang of well-dressed upper-class students. They, at least, should have known better than to taunt and tease the porters who moved surefootedly through the crowd with sometimes as many as ten baskets balanced on their heads. The young men were drunk, yes, but couldn't they still act a little like gentlemen? At least while I was looking?

Overcome with disillusion, I muttered to myself, "I'll go back to the ship."

But as I turned to leave, slender fingers clutched my arm so suddenly I jerked back, afraid I might be about to be beaten up and robbed while the crowd looked on with indifference.

No, it was a young lady who had grabbed my arm so firmly. Was she a prostitute? She didn't look like one, with her bonnet, her long skirts, her shawl, her obviously corseted middle. Her clothes were those of the middle class, perhaps even the lower upper, and she wore no makeup. And that pale perfect skin in her cheeks, that expression of innocent fear! She was a lady indeed, though not much over twenty-one.

"What's this?" I asked her awkwardly, as she tugged wordlessly at my arm. "What do you want?"

At last she managed to speak. "Oh help me, sir! Help me! *Don't let them get me!*"

CHAPTER 8

I tried to put her on a passing horse-drawn omnibus, but she wouldn't hear of that. "They'll follow me. They'll attack me on the bus!" she cried.

So I hailed a hansom cab. "Tell the driver your address," I said, as she climbed in.

"Aren't you coming with me?"

"Well. . . ."

"You must!"

"The driver will protect you."

"No, no, they'll pay him off and he'll look the other way while they drag me into the street!" It was she who was actually doing the dragging, clutching my arm with a strength quite surprising in such a dainty girl. I gave in. After all, what harm could it do?

I threw my duffle bag in the cab and climbed up onto the seat beside her. She slammed the half-doors in front of us herself, then called out an address to the stoic, top-hatted driver seated behind and above us. "Giddy-up, Victoria," he grunted, with a thick cockney accent, and we set off across the cobblestones at a brisk clippity-clop. The lanterns on either side of the cab were lit, and I could see the horse's tail clearly enough, but the ears were lost in the fog. Nevertheless the driver did not hesitate, navigating through oblivion as if by some bat-sonar unknown to ordinary mortals. In the market (which was roofed-over though open on all four sides) the many lanterns had somewhat thinned the fog, but here it ruled in undisputed mastery. All the same the girl insisted on leaning dangerously far out of the cab and peering back the way we had come, though an entire army of rapists and murderers could have ben there and we wouldn't have seen them. "I don't see them," she said inanely.

I wondered who "they" might be. Professor Moriarty and his gang? Or Jack the Ripper?

"I think," I began uneasily, "you owe me some sort of explanation, Miss. . . ."

"My name is Mary Arthur."

"Mine is Newton McClintok."

We shook hands with a formality that, under the circumstances, seemed utterly absurd, but her desperate

Then Beggars Could Ride

expression as she gazed at me in the light from the cablamps forced me to take it seriously.

"Don't hate me," she said, pleadingly.

"Why should I hate you?"

"I've put you in danger. You understand, don't you, that I had no choice? You were the only one in Covent Garden Market who had an honest look about him, and you're a sailor, too."

"What difference does it make if I'm a sailor?"

"Well, everyone knows a sailor does his duty, come what may, and that they're ever so brave."

I wondered silently if she'd ever known a real sailor personally, but I agreed, "Yes, I suppose that's true."

"You're strong, too," she added shyly, touching my arm. Thanks to the life I'd been leading recently, there was something there worth touching.

"Miss Arthur—"

"You must call me Mary. I'm a modern girl, you know." This was said quite firmly.

"Mary, if I'm going to be any use at all to you, you've got to tell me who it is you're so afraid of, and what I can expect from them."

"Expect anything! There's no trick too low for them. I'm frightened, Sailor. Hold me!" I put my arm around her shoulders.

"Tighter!" she commanded.

"How's that?" I gave her a squeeze.

"Oh, much better, thank you." Her voice was calmer. Through the layers of clothing I could feel her supple flesh. It reminded me forcefully that I had not had a woman since I'd left Chaplin.

I prompted, "You were saying, about 'Them'?"

"Irish revolutionaries! Depraved Fenians! They kidnapped me in broad daylight two days ago, from right in front of my father's house! I was with the downstairs maid. They clubbed her and left her lying in the street, her head cut open to the bone. For all I know, she may be dead!" Here I was afraid Mary might break into tears, but she only sucked in her breath and continued. "Oh, sir, it was dreadful! They've not the least regard for human life! They threw me into a coach and spirited me away before anyone could give chase. And as we raced along, one of them tied my hands and feet while the other gagged me and blindfolded me; a third held a dagger to my throat and threatened, if I struggled or cried out, to slit my gullet like a chicken's. He was a farm boy, I think, from the way he talked. Certainly not a gentleman!" Her fear was giving way to righteous indignation.

"Go on," I urged, still holding her tightly around the shoulders. The fog was lightening. Dawn must be coming on. I could make out the outlines of the nearest buildings.

"It was frightful, sir! They were so rough with me. And the language they used!" This business of the language seemed to be the worst part of the whole experience, to judge from her tone of mortified shock. "I am a modern girl, as I've said, but there must be a limit! They locked me in a windowless room, not far, as it turned out, from the Covent Garden Market. They made me write a note to my papa, asking for ransom money—the money, they told me, was for bombs to blow up the New Scotland Yard the same as they blew up the old one—and then, sir, they told me that they would kill me even if they got the money, for I'd seen their faces, you know."

To calm her, I said, "But you are alive and free now."

"Yes, yes, but no thanks to them. I escaped, you see."

"Escaped? How?"

"You know how it is with the Irish and strong drink. Disgraceful!"

"I suppose so."

"But this time the *spiritus fermenti* saved a life instead of ruining one. We should be thankful perhaps that *Quae fuerunt vitia, mores sunt*."

"You speak Latin?" I said, surprised.

"And Greek, too!" she answered with a touch of vanity, then, to demonstrate, lapsed into a torrent of Greek.

"The kidnappers!" I interrupted. "Tell me how you got away from the kidnappers."

"Oh. Simple. The rascals began drinking toasts to the downfall of the Queen and other such wicked things, then they went away, all but the one left to guard me. This guard was, by this time, so drunk he forgot to lock my door, and when, after a bit, he passed out, I sneaked out and ran for it . . . then I saw you."

"Don't worry," I said soothingly. "I'm sure you're safe now."

She looked up at me with wide, trusting eyes. "You're sure?"

"This fog has certainly covered your escape."

Then Beggars Could Ride

She continued to gaze up at me, moist lips slightly parted. I looked at the lips for a long silent moment.

Then I kissed them.

She struggled weakly at first, then changed her mind and returned the kiss with enthusiasm. We went on kissing for over a minute.

When we pulled apart she seemed upset, and when she could speak, muttered, "Oh dear. Oh dear."

"I'm sorry," I said, embarrassed.

"No, it's not your fault. I never should have encouraged you. You are, after all, only a man, poor thing."

"I guess you're right," I agreed, and tried to kiss her again.

She pushed me away. "The fog is lifting," she whispered. "People will see. My reputation. . . ."

I glanced around. I could actually read the lettering on the signs we passed and see the other hansom cabs that passed us going in the other direction.

"Your arm." she said urgently.

I took my arm reluctantly from around her shoulders.

A bootblack on a streetcorner looked up at us with a startled expression and tipped his cap.

Mary was alarmed. "That boy! Did he see you with your arm around me?"

"I don't think so."

"Oh, dear, oh dear, I hope not." She was biting her nails. "He knows me. He does papa's boots, you know. And he's a little snitch if ever there was one."

The hansom cab came to a stop. The driver called down, "Here's your address, Miss." She and I climbed down. I left my bag on the cab floor, expecting to jump back in as soon as I saw her to her door. She paid the fare, which was fortunate, considering how little money I had, then turned toward her house.

Then she stopped, frozen.

"There's nobody home," she whispered, alarmed.

The building we faced was a three-story angular Victorian gothic town house, fairly new and luxuriously decorated. It was set back from the street and had two large apple trees in the front yard. The windows were dark, but at this hour that was hardly surprising.

"Maybe there is somebody there," I suggested. "Some servants, maybe." It was the kind of house that one associates with servants.

"I daren't go in alone," she said.

We stood indecisively while the early morning light grew rapidly brighter.

"Make up yer minds," said the driver, annoyed. "Will y'be wantin' a cab or won't ye?"

"Get your bag," she told me firmly.

I obeyed.

"You may go now, my man," she said to the driver.

"Thank you, Miss." He clucked his tongue and the hansom rattled away.

"Now look sharp," she said. "Those villains may have come back here to get me. They'd guess this was the first place I'd go." I followed her up a short flight of steps to a narrow front porch.

"How will we get in?" I asked worriedly.

"I've a key." She drew a key on the end of a string up out of the inside of her white lace bodice. "Hush now." She unlocked the front door, pushed it open. It squeaked.

When we were inside, she very quietly closed it and locked it behind us.

I whispered, "Maybe you'd better call out something. You know, 'I'm home, folks!' Or something like that."

"Don't be a ninny," she whispered back. "If the Irishmen are here, that'll bring them down on our necks in a second. Come along. Follow me."

We crossed an imposing hall, two floors tall, and tiptoed up a circular marble staircase. On the second floor I saw gaslight fixtures on the walls, but she did not light them, preferring to grope along the dark hallway and up the narrow back stairs to the third floor. At this point she turned to me, finger on lips, and whispered, "This is my room."

She opened a door and we quickly slipped inside.

I looked around.

In the morning light I could see everything quite plainly. There were the bookcases with the books whose titles were in Latin, Greek and French as well as English; the bed, with ornate brass bedstead and a navy-blue quilt neatly covering it; the marble-topped dresser with its porcelain pitcher and basin; the matching bedtable; an overstuffed chair. All these things were exactly what I would have expected. But on top of the bookcase, stood the detailed model of an eighteenth-century British ship-of-the-line, complete with tiny sails and tiny sailors. And

Then Beggars Could Ride

on the walls hung eight framed lithographs, in color, of famous sailing ships. I suddenly felt very uneasy.

"Well," she demanded, gesturing around the room, "What do you think of it?" Her voice was still low, as if she was afraid of being overheard.

"Nice."

"But?"

"But—now don't take this wrong—it doesn't look like a girl's room. I mean, where's the dolls, the flowers, the frills?"

"I don't care for that sort of thing," she answered with disdain. She took off her shawl and her bonnet and threw them on the chair.

"Why not?"

"You wouldn't understand. You're a man. You can do what you like, be what you like. The world was made for you and you for the world." All trace of the fear she had showed a moment earlier had vanished. Instead she now fixed me with a disquietingly calculating eye. "You like the way things are in Sherlock, don't you?"

"More or less."

"Of course you do. And why not? Here you have everything your own way." She was reaching behind her, unbuttoning her lace bodice. "Help me undo these buttons, will you?" Her voice was almost angry. Uncertainly I obeyed.

"It's not because I'm a man. It's because I'm attracted by order, tradition, decency. These things mean as much to a woman as to a man," I said.

"Lies!" she snapped. Her bodice joined her bonnet and shawl on the overstuffed chair. "Balderdash!"

"What are you doing?" I demanded apprehensively.

"What does it look like, you ninny? I'm getting undressed. I thought I ought to start before you did, because I have more to take off." She had begun to undo her long skirt. "Didn't it ever occur to you a woman might want something else? Freedom? Adventure?" She had raised her voice.

I said nervously, "Not so loud. The Irishmen might—"

"Don't you understand yet, you silly thing? There aren't any Irishmen. There never were." Her skirt slid to the floor and she stepped out of it, but under it she had a white muslin petticoat.

"I'd better be going," I said lamely, starting for the door.

"There aren't any Irishmen," she said, "But there are parents and servants. They're all around us. If I were to scream—"

"No, no, don't do that," I said hastily, turning back toward her. I was remembering what I'd read in the paper about the man who'd seduced a girl of Good Family. He'd gotten the death penalty.

"Now you're being reasonable," she said with satisfaction. "You see, there's only one thing you can do now."

"And what's that?"

"Love me," she whispered, but her voice was more sad than triumphant. There was a long pause as she struggled with her corset. Then she added, "And help me get out of this bloody corset!" She stood, arms akimbo, and glared at me. Her hair, which had been done up in a bun at the nape of her neck, had come undone and cascaded, long, unruly and blond, over her narrow shoulders all the way to her small firm breasts whose curving outlines were clearly visible under her embroidered chemise. Below her waist she now wore nothing but billowing bloomers, long stockings and high button shoes. The toe of her right shoe began to tap impatiently. "I have a maid who usually helps me," she said in a low voice. "Shall I call her?"

"No, I'll do it." I threw down my duffle bag and stepped toward her.

When I'd gotten the corset off, she said, "You must have a lot of practice wtih ladies' corsets, you did that so easily. You sailors are dreadfully naughty, aren't you?"

"So they say." Such a feeling of tenderness had come over me I could hardly speak.

"I'm experienced too, in my way," she said, closing her eyes and raising her lips to be kissed.

But that was another of her lies. I found, a half an hour later, that she was—or had been—a virgin.

I TRIED to stay awake and wait for my chance to escape, but instead I slept and did not even dream.

It was, from the slant of the light, afternoon when I reluctantly opened my eyes again. Mary was shaking my shoulder roughly, saying in an urgent voice, "Wake up, Sailor. Wake up."

Then Beggars Could Ride

She turned her head, looked away from me. I followed the line of her gaze.

At the foot of the bed stood a portly gentleman in mutton-chop whiskers and a smoking jacket. In his right hand he held a Smith and Wesson revolver, not pointing it directly at me, but in my general direction.

Mary's voice shook only slightly—she was, after all, a modern girl—as she said with stiff formality, "Mr. Sailor, I'd like you to meet my father, Sir James Arthur, late of Her Majesty's Northumberland Fusiliers."

CHAPTER 9

"Inspector Lestrade? This is Sir James. Yes, good to talk to you again, old boy." He lowered the telephone receiver a moment to give me a warning frown. I had dared to put down my duffle bag. He went on, "I've a bit of a problem over here. A degenerate—American, I think—molesting little Mary. You remember Mary, of course. Yes. The tomboy. Could you nip over here and escort him to jail? That's a good fellow! He'll be here when you arrive, never fear."

With that Sir James hung up.

He had allowed Mary and me to dress, and now we three stood glaring at each other in the front hall at the foot of the circular staircase, next to the telephone table. He had not for one instant put down his revolver, and now he used it to gesture toward some nearby sliding doors.

"We'll wait in the drawing room, if you don't mind," he said, bowing slightly.

With a sigh I shouldered my duffle and entered the room he'd indicated, Mary at my side and Sir James behind me. "Do be seated," he said, sliding the doors shut. "Lestrade will be here shortly. As you may have gathered, the Inspector is an old friend. Yes, an old friend of the family. Many's the time he's bounced little Mary on his knee." His voice shook with controlled emotion, and his face was brick red.

I sat down on a large, richly carved sofa upholstered in maroon silk damask. Mary sat on a matching rocking chair on my right. Her father remained standing, pacing back and forth in front of us. The heavy curtains on the windows were only slightly open, leaving it quite dim, but not dim enough, unfortunately, to impede Sir James's marksmanship. There was a musty smell in the room, as if it were not often used, and the air was hot and humid. On the walls hung oil paintings, portraits of frowning gentlemen in uniforms who all bore a family resemblance to Sir James.

Mr. Arthur showed no inclination to talk, but after a moment Mary spoke up. "Must you be so beastly about it, Papa?"

Then Beggars Could Ride

"I? Beastly?" He was dangerously close to losing his temper.

"Yes, Papa. This is no way to treat your future son-in-law."

He stopped his pacing and turned a still deeper shade of red, his eyes bulging as if he was on the verge of a fit. When he could speak he said, "You're insane. You always were an imaginative child, and now at last. . . ." He could not go on.

"I'll have you know I'd consider it an honor to be called Mrs. . . ." She faltered, trying to remember my name. I silently wished her luck. "Mrs. Jones," she said brightly. "Mr. Bobby Jones has asked for my hand, and I've said yes."

Mr. Arthur's voice was that of someone humoring a lunatic. "He is a bit old for you, don't you think?"

"I like maturity in a man." (It was quite possible that I was older than her father.)

"And his family—"

"He comes from excellent family. He's not the first well-born boy forced by unfortunate circumstances to go to sea." She was lying with such conviction that Bobby Jones had begun to take shape in my mind, to seem like my real identity.

"Unfortunate circumstances?" he echoed. "If he is in unfortunate circumstances, how in bloody hell do you think he will support you?"

"Oh, we have that all figured out, Papa."

"Indeed?"

"Oh yes. He will take me with him on his ship."

"The devil you say!"

"I'll disguise myself as a man, like the girl in that old song 'Jackaroe', and sign on as cabin boy," she said firmly. I wondered how long she'd had this idea in her mind. Had she improvised it this very moment, or had it been in her mind back in the Covent Garden Market, before she grabbed my arm? Had it been in her mind even earlier, when she'd hung the ship pictures on her walls and built the model of the British ship-of-the-line with the loving care most young ladies in this city probably lavished on their needlework?

He turned to me. "Mr. Jones?"

"Yes, sir," I said promptly.

"Is this true?"

Doc had said a moment would come when I would be presented with a list of names from which to choose a new identity. He hadn't said the list would contain only one name. I realized that it was not yet too late to say, "No, I'm not Bobby Jones. My name is Newton McClintok." I glanced at Mary. There was a desperate pleading look in her eyes. She was a lovely creature, though unbelievably naive, and intelligent, probably a good deal more intelligent than I. And she was bold. Being with her might be painful—I'd never know when she was telling me the truth—but it would not be dull. I said, "Yes, sir. It's true."

She squeezed my hand. "Oh, Bobby," she whispered, delighted.

"You're a cad, sir," said Sir James.

"Perhaps."

"And a bounder!"

"Possibly, but love makes a man do strange things." I didn't sound right to myself. I would have to study the art of falsehood. Mary would teach me.

"You say you love Mary?"

"Yes, sir." The sharp tenderness struck me again, as it had in her room. Maybe I really did love her. The idea was frightening.

"And you want to marry her?"

Newton McClintok couldn't marry anyone. He was already married, to Marge. But Bobby Jones wasn't married. "Yes, sir," I said.

He said quietly, "I think I'll kill you now." He took aim at my forehead. "Now, before things get too complicated. No court in Sherlock would convict me."

"You always wanted a son!" Mary said sharply.

"What?" he said vaguely. The gun wavered.

Her voice was triumphant. "I'm giving you a son! That's more than Mama was ever able to do!"

He lowered the gun. His round features collapsed in baffled frustration, confusion, uncertainty. There was fear there, too. He was afraid of his daughter. Perhaps with reason.

The door to the drawing room slid open and a stately matron in a dark green ankle-length skirt and polka-dot blouse peered in, blinking. "What's going on in here?" she demanded, then she saw the revolver. "My word! James! Do put that ugly thing away. You might hurt someone."

Then Beggars Could Ride

Mary sprang up and ran to her. "Mama! Mama! He's going to kill my fiancé!"

The woman embraced. "Good grief, James!" cried Mrs. Arthur, appalled. "Have you taken leave of your senses?"

"I won't shoot him," grumbled Mr. Arthur, but there was disappointment in his voice. "I'm just holding him here until Mr. Lestrade comes."

"Lestrade? The police officer?" said Mrs. Arthur.

"Bobby came to ask for my hand," said Mary, burying her head in her mother's ample bosom. "And now Papa's going to have him arrested."

"Surely not, dear. Surely not." Her voice was soothing. "It's all a misunderstanding. We'll sit down and discuss it rationally and. . . ." She squinted at me in the dim light. "Please excuse us, young man. My husband is rather excitable."

"I am not!" Mr. Arthur objected indignantly.

"His name is Bobby Jones," said Mary to her mother.

"Ah, I'm delighted to know you, Mr. Jones." The matron stepped gracefully toward me, extending her hand.

Sir James snapped. "That will be enough, woman!"

She stopped. I had half-risen to shake her hand and now sank back on the couch.

"Sit down, dear." He had taken a commanding tone with his wife, and after an instant's hesitation, she obeyed. "That's better!" He spoke more calmly now. "After Inspector Lestrade leaves, we will discuss the matter. Until then we will wait. Is that understood?"

"Yes, dear," said his wife with resignation.

The room fell silent. I became aware of the muffled sound of horses and coaches passing in the street outside.

"Papa." Mary began. She was once again seated to my right.

"Not a word!" commanded her father.

"But—"

"I will send you to your room if you speak again," he said fiercely.

After another long silence I heard a wagon stop in front of the house.

"That will be Lestrade," he said, relieved.

Footsteps sounded on the front stairs. Judging from the racket they made, there were three or four men. The heavy door knocker thumped. There was a long pause, then it thumped again.

"Where's that confounded butler?" demanded Mr. Arthur.

"It's his day off, I believe," answered Mrs. Arthur.

"Well, what about the downstairs maid?" he asked, getting angry all over again.

"I'm sure I wouldn't know," Mrs. Arthur replied.

"Damn and blast!" shouted Mr. Arthur as the door knocker thumped a third time. The last shred of his composure had vanished, "Do I have to answer the door myself?"

"So it would appear, dear," said his wife.

He thrust the revolver into her hands, roaring. "All right, then! I'll answer it! And you take this gun, and if that sailor makes one move, blow his head off!"

He stormed out into the hall, calling, "I'm coming! I'm coming!"

Mrs. Arthur stared at the weapon in her hand with horror and distaste, then she looked at me. I could hear the front door being unlocked.

Abruptly Mrs. Arthur threw the gun into a chair and whispered urgently, "Out the back door, children! Quick! Run!"

My impulse, when we had had reached the back yard, was to keep on running; it was Mary who opened the ample woodbox, jumped nimbly inside, and fiercely gestured for me to do the same.

We were inside the box with the top closed when Mr. Arthur sprinted past, puffing and panting and shouting, "This way, Lestrade! They went this way!" Lestrade and his men passed an instant later, also, from the sound of it, running at top speed.

The minute the back gate, which apparently led into an alley, banged shut behind the policemen, Mary popped out of the box and bounded to the ground.

"Where to now?" I asked, scrambling out after her.

"Into the house. But don't let Mama get a close look at you. She thinks you're a young fellow. If she sees how old you actually are, she may go over to Papa's side. Keep away from her now, and don't worry. Her eyesight is none too good."

Mrs. Arthur was amazed when we burst in on her. She was still standing in the front hall, at the foot of the circular staircase. "Oh Mary, you're back!" she cried.

Then Beggars Could Ride

"Only for a moment, Mama." Mary kissed her mother briefly on the cheek.

"Perhaps you'll need some money—" began the older woman.

"I have money, Mama. Just give me your blessing."

"You know you have that, dear. And after you're properly married, you can come back. Your father will accept it in time. He has great respect for the institution of marriage."

"Goodbye, Mama."

"Goodbye, dear." Mrs. Arthur had begun to cry. She turned her gaze in my direction, but I thanked God her vision was even more than usually impaired by those overflowing tears. I had to pass quite close to her as I followed Mary to the front door, close enough to hear her murmur softly, "A sailor! How romantic!"

As Mary and I emerged from the house, I nearly turned around and ran back inside. Parked at the curb stood a four-wheel, two-horse coach painted black with no windows on the sides and the doors at the back. There were windows in these doors, windows with bars in them. It was the Black Maria, here to cart me off to prison. A bored uniformed policeman leaned against the cast-iron horse's head hitching post to which the horses were tethered.

Mary did not hesitate, but ran straight to him.

"Inspector Lestrade told me to tell you to come quick," she cried breathlessly. "He needs you, out back."

He touched his cap. "Thank you kindly, Miss." He ran up the front steps, hardly glancing at me.

The officer was no sooner out of sight when Mary began to untie the horses from the hitching post.

"What are you doing now?" I demanded, horrified.

"Stealing the Black Maria, of course." In a swirl of skirts she mounted to the driver's seat at the front of the coach. "Are you coming, or shall I leave you behind?"

I heard angry shouts from behind the house, and scrambled up beside her. She gave the reins a vigorous shake and the horses set off at a canter. I was depositing my duffle under the seat when I heard a howl of dismay behind me. I turned and saw Mr. Arthur standing, open-mouthed, in his front doorway, with Lestrade, equally amazed, beside him. It was only a glimpse, then the Black

Maria rounded a corner and our pursuers were lost from view.

"How could you do it?" I said. "How could you steal the police's own coach?"

"It was the rational thing to do. We obtain transportation for ourselves and deprive our enemies of it, all at a single stroke." She had the whip out now and was urging the horses to a gallop.

"The rational thing to do?" I echoed weakly. We rounded a corner so fast the coach nearly overturned. "Not so fast there!"

She explained patiently. "We must go as fast as possible, Bobby. The coppers will certainly commandeer some sort of vehicle and be after us in a twinkling." I hung on as we swerved to avoid a pushcart. The vendor who owned the cart shook his fist at us and shouted blasphemies.

"Let's head for the West India docks," I suggested. "That's where my ship is berthed."

She shook her head firmly. "No, no, they know you're a sailor. That's the first place they'll look for us." We had raised our voices to almost a shout to make ourselves heard over the thunder of the horses' hooves and the clatter of the careening carriage.

"Then where?" I demanded.

She was puzzled, but not for long. "I know!" she exclaimed with delight. She turned her wild eyes toward me, and I thought I saw more than a hint of madness in them.

"To the future!" she cried.

WE abandoned the Black Maria in a side street and proceeded for six blocks on foot, finding ourselves at last, somewhat winded by our forced march, in front of a two-story red brick house with an attached greenhouse. Mary confidently stepped up to the front door and gave the bell cord a pull.

After a moment the door was opened by a gaunt, pale little man in his early twenties with a sparse mustache and innocent, yet somehow mocking, blue eyes. He did not look very healthy, and in spite of the heat of the afternoon, wore a sweater under his vest and suitcoat. The impression of ill-health was reinforced by his habit of raising his bony fist to his lips and coughing discreetly every minute or so.

Then Beggars Could Ride

"Mary!" he said, with a broad cockney accent. "Well now, this is a pleasant surprise. Come in, come in!"

He led us into a shabby but clean and respectable living room, unusual only in the inordinate number of well-stocked bookcases. "Do be seated," he said, after one of his little coughs. "The missis is out shopping this afternoon. She'll be sorry to have missed you."

Mary explained, for my benefit, "His wife was a classmate of mine." She giggled.

When I looked puzzled, he said, "You might as well know the whole story. Everyone else does."

Mary said with excited admiration, "Herbert here" she gestured toward the man, who sat smiling at us from across the coffee table. "Herbert was my teacher, you see, before he left his dull little wife and ran off with one of his students, who happened to be one of my best friends."

"There was quite a scandal at the time," he said, with an odd touch of pride in his voice. "It put an end to my teaching career."

"I can imagine," I said. It was hard to concentrate on what he was saying. Instead I kept thinking about Mr. Arthur and Inspector Lestrade. By this time they must have set the entire Metropolitan Police Force looking for us.

Mary, however, gossiped on. "Forgive me, Herbert. I forgot to introduce you. This is my fiancé, Bobby Jones."

"An honor, sir," he said as we shook hands. He had a disturbingly weak handshake.

"We're eloping," she confided melodramatically.

"Oh, capital," he chuckled, then broke into a brief fit of coughing.

"But I need your help," she added, in a more serious tone.

"My help? What on earth could I do?"

"We must get out of Sherlock, and quickly. I thought if I could use your machine. . . ."

"My machine?" He frowned. "I don't know."

"Oh please, Herbert! You, of all people, must know it's a matter of life and death!"

"Very well," he agreed reluctantly, as he got up. "It's in the greenhouse."

He led the way.

In the greenhouse, among the potted plants and gardening tools, he showed us a curious carriage-like contraption fitted out with all sorts of wires and dials. "Get in," he told us, bowing slightly.

"This isn't going to get us anywhere," I protested. "It doesn't have any wheels!"

"Don't be a ninny, Bob," she snapped, clambering into the weird machine. She patted the seat next to her. "I'm waiting." From the tone of her voice I knew there was no use arguing, so I got in and sat down.

"Throw the switch, Herbert," she called cheerily.

"Righto!" He closed a huge knife-switch on the wall.

She grasped my hand, but I was nevertheless uneasy enough to mutter, "Mary, I don't even know who this Herbert fellow is. Suppose that—"

She broke in, "He's only my dear old teacher, Herbert George Wells. You may have seen his stories in the magazines. He writes scientific romances under the name H.G. Wells."

All around us brilliant colored lights were flashing and wisps of smoke rising. The air was filled with the bitter aroma of ozone and from deep within the machine came a frightful wail, louder and louder, higher and higher, until I was afraid my eardrums would burst.

CHAPTER 10

"It wasn't really a time machine at all," I cried.

"Well, of course not," said Mary as we hurried along the dimly lit underground tunnel. "There's no such thing as a real time machine. It was a good mim, though, wasn't it?"

After Wells had thrown the switch we had not gone zooming off into the future. Instead the floor under the so-called time machine had slowly descended like an elevator down a deep shaft, howling and buzzing and throwing sparks all the way, finally coming to rest at a doorway that opened into the subterranean passageway in which we now found ourselves. There was a disconcerting echo, and here and there along the walls a tall brown water stain was etched; there was no actual water in sight, but the air was cold and damp.

"But if it wasn't a real time machine, why did you say we were going to the future?" I demanded.

"You'll see, Bobby dear."

We turned a corner that opened into yet another tunnel, much larger than the first. As we entered this larger tunnel, I looked around in bewilderment. "What is this, Mary?"

"It's a subway station. Monorail." She pointed to a T-shaped rail that ran along the roof to vanish in the distance both to my right and to my left. There were no tracks on the floor. "It's the Los Angeles Rapid Transit System."

She pressed a button on the wall. A small red light above it snapped on.

"And now what are you doing?" I asked her.

"I have to notify the train I'm here."

"Wouldn't the driver see you?"

"There is no driver. The train's totally automated."

I was beginning to understand what she meant about escaping into the future. She leaned casually against the wall. "This is actually a maintenance stop. It's hardly ever used except by Herbert. Herbert loves to ride the train all over, to mims of all sorts of times and places. In a way, you see, he does have a time machine."

"But what's this train doing here?" I set down my duffle.

"We must have at least some transportation, mustn't

we? And the techs wouldn't allow coal-burning locomotives, so we have dummy rail stations on the surface and the real trains—electric ones—down here. Listen! We're in luck. There's one coming already."

Far away a faint roaring sound had become audible, and now it grew and grew.

"Look!" she exclaimed delightedly, pointing.

A single headlight had appeared in the distance and bore down on us with surprising speed. The roaring grew, but never became as loud as I expected; the train was rolling on rubber tires, almost like a trailer-truck turned upside down. As it came near us it slowed and stopped without a trace of a jerk; the doors in the first segment slid open with a swish.

"Hurry," she said, springing through the doorway. "It won't wait forever."

I snatched up my duffle and followed her in, and the doors closed themselves behind us. I noticed, as the train got underway, that all the seats on our car were empty, including that of the driver up front. It gave me an eerie feeling, as if we'd boarded a ghost train, not to mention that I'd never ridden a train of any kind before. All the same, in the brief glimpse I'd caught of it, the car we were in had looked oddly familiar. Had I seen a picture of it somewhere? In Doc's office perhaps? When we were seated, I asked Mary about it.

She laughed. "This train is a pretty close mim of the one that used to take people to Disneyland, before the Year of the Great Cold. I'm not surprised your tech friend had a picture of it. You know, don't you, that Walt Disney once offered to build Los Angeles a rapid transit system. His Disneyland train was a pilot model. Those fools on the city government turned him down. They were afraid, I suppose, the main station would be at Disneyland." She sighed. "Poor old Walt. He must have been lonely. A twenty-first century man marooned in the twentieth century. Now, of course, the system he planned has actually been built, though he didn't live to see it. For that matter, the whole world has been turned into one big Disneyland!"

I was amazed by Mary's knowledge. She couldn't possibly have learned all this in school in Sherlock, where the name of Walt Disney would not be mentioned. Perhaps such knowledge was bootlegged from child to child, as it

Then Beggars Could Ride

had been in Chaplin . . . though bootlegged information was notoriously unreliable.

When I asked her about it, she told me, "Well, I've traveled, you see. I've been all over Los Angeles with Herbert. Though you needn't tell his wife, Herbert is rather stuck on me. Did you notice? I've been to all the uptime mims, even"—here her voice dropped to an awed whisper—"even Disneyland itself. It doesn't cost anything to ride the trains, but nobody rides them, as you can see."

I ventured, "Maybe there are people on the other cars."

She laughed. "This is the only passenger car in the train. The others are containerized freight cars."

"But your classmates, your parents . . . don't they ever get curious? Don't they ever wonder what might be going on in the next enclave?"

She turned to me angrily and snapped, "Don't act like such a dunce! You know what people are like!"

That stopped me. I certainly did know what people were like.

Suddenly she burst out, "Bobby, Bobby! Get ready. We're getting off at the next station." The train was slowing so smoothly I had not been aware of it.

The car was flooded with light, almost blinding me. The doors opened and we stumbled out. I wondered, *What kind of a crazy enclave have we blundered into this time?*

"Welcome to Futuria," said the ten-foot-tall Tin Woodsman of Oz.

THE sun had set, but the Grand Concourse was lit bright as day by banks of floodlights on the walls of the tall chrome and glass buildings that stood to my right and to my left; lights that turned the concourse into a kind of shimmering artificial canyon stretching out ahead of me, straight as a ruler line, for at least a mile. The habits of a lifetime brought a question almost involuntarily to my lips. "How can they waste so much power?"

Mary laughed. "This is Futuria! They have a geothermal energy plant here that reaches into the depths of the Earth and brings up more energy than they can possibly use, and they don't have to share it with anyone. Let's go!"

She led me by the hand out onto the moving sidewalk, dancing nimbly from the slow-moving outer belts to the faster inner ones.

"That Tin Woodsman," I said as we breezed along. "Was he a mechanical man?"

"A robot? Yes. And also a remote in-out terminal for the computer that controls this whole enclave. Wasn't it keen the way he answered my question, directing us to the nearest hotel?"

"Spooky," I answered with a shudder.

She gave me a playful punch in the arm. "Why can't you be modern, like me?"

There were few other people on the moving sidewalks; an occasional small group in various-colored tech coveralls ... mostly white, with some blues and greens. Fewer still "civilians" dressed in simple bright-colored knee-length nylon tricot shifts with floral borders on the hems, some barefoot, some with soft plastic boots in colors to match their shifts. It was difficult to tell the males from the females, since all dressed in the same style and all had crew cuts.

"Where is everyone?" I asked.

"There aren't many people living here." She gestured toward the gleaming glass facades we were passing. "Most of these buildings are vacant."

"But why?"

"Well, Futuria is such a dreadful bore, you see."

Ahead of us and to the right a ten-story neon sign blinked red and yellow alternately. It said, "Jules Verne Hotel." Only then did I realize how dead-tired I was, how glad I'd be to collapse into a warm, comfortable bed. We started toward the slower, outer belts, moving quickly so as not to overshoot the hotel.

"Oh oh," Mary said in a worried voice.

I saw what was worrying her.

A bald-headed tech in pale blue coveralls was running toward us across the outer belts. He was an old guy, but from the way he was running, he seemed in excellent physical condition.

"A plain clothes copper!" Mary snapped and began running back toward the fastest inner belt. I ran too, though every bone in my body protested.

"Newton!" called the man. "Newton McClintok!"

I thought, *He must be a cop all right. How else would he know me by that name?*

"Stop!" he shouted. "Please! I want to help you."

Then Beggars Could Ride

I thought, *Sure you do, buster,* and ran even faster.

He was behind us now, on the fastest belt. "Doc sent me!" he added, between puffs and pants. His age was beginning to tell. It looked like we'd get away from him.

Then Mary tripped on her skirts and fell sprawling with a squeal of frustration and despair. "Damn and blast!" she cried, in an unconscious mim of her father.

I stopped and ran back to help her, but the tech reached her first, lifting her to her feet with gentlemanly courtesy. I had heard that the officers of Scotland Yard carried no firearms. Hoping that was true, I balled my fists and growled, "Let her go, Copper."

His face was flushed and he was so winded he could hardly speak, but he managed to blurt out, "I'm . . . not a . . . copper. No, no. Honest I'm not." He sucked in a deep breath. "But there *will* be coppers here . . . any minute. We've got to get you off the streets. With those clothes . . . you stick out like a sore thumb."

I hesitated. He hadn't snapped the handcuffs on us. He hadn't arrested us. Maybe he was telling the truth.

"Liar," Mary muttered. She took a step away from him. He made no move to stop her. That decided me.

"No," I told her. "He's telling the truth."

He heaved a tremendous sigh of relief, then wheezed, "Quick! Follow me!"

THE floor-to-ceiling picture windows in the elevator were tinted so that we could see out but nobody could see in, at least not clearly. As the elevator glided smoothly up the outer face of the building, I saw the short, unmistakable figure of Inspector Lestrade, together with a squad of uniformed officers from the Yard, come riding the moving sidewalk far below us, crossing the outer belts in time to disembark at the front entrance to the Jules Verne Hotel.

I turned to the blue-coveralled tech and said, "I don't know how you did it, but you sure saved our skins. Thanks, pal!" I shook his hand vigorously.

Mary said nothing, her expression still showing more suspicion than gratitude.

The elevator slowed to a stop; the doors opened.

We stepped into a long narrow hallway lit with soft shadowless indirect lighting and carpeted with the richest, deepest wall-to-wall rug I'd ever seen. Some invisible loudspeakers were playing gentle but very strange music, moaning, seductive. I was certain there were more than twelve tones to the octave, and the rhythm had no metronomic beat, but ebbed and flowed like ocean waves. Strangest of all was the melody, inhumanly subtle, depending on changes of pitch so infinitesimal the ear could hardly detect them.

"This way," the tech said.

I noticed, as we went along the passageway, that the doors, which were spaced at considerable intervals, were perfectly smooth. There was no sign of any sort of doorknob, though beside each doorway there was a round flat disk I at first took to be a doorbell. The tech noticed my curiosity and explained, "They're thumbprint readers. The door won't open for you unless your thumbprint is in its memory banks."

He stopped in front of one of the doors and pressed his thumb against the reader. With a swish the door slid open and, when we had entered, closed itself again. The weird whispering music was playing here too, until he touched another disk, making it stop, plunging the room into a silence so profound I could hear my own heartbeat.

"Have a seat," he said. His voice, now that he had regained his breath, was deep and confident.

"Thanks," I said. The chair changed its shape to exactly fit the contours of my body, almost as if it were a living thing. Mary sat in another, identical chair on my left. The chairs pulsed faintly, as if breathing.

"I won't offer you any alcoholic refreshment." He rocked on his heels, smiling down on us. "I understand, Newton, that you have a problem that way. But you must be hungry, both of you. Can I get you something to eat?"

I thought a moment, then said, "How about a hot dog and a chocolate milk shake?"

He laughed. "It'll have to be something a little less typical of your time and place of origin. I'm calling down to the kitchen for it, and Lestrade will check the kitchens for just such slip ups. How about a steak with potatoes, eh?"

"Fine," I agreed.

"And Mary, what will you have?" he asked her.

"I'm not hungry, thank you all the same," she answered in a low voice.

The tech went into the next room, probably to order

the food. I whispered to Mary, "Why aren't you eating?"

She whispered back, "Because the food may be drugged."

"Don't be silly."

"Silly, am I? Tell me, if the door won't open without this fellow's thumbprint, how would you go about leaving this room?" I got up and looked around. There was a picture window, but it looked out on a sheer drop of perhaps thirteen floors. One window and one door, and the door only opened for the Right People.

Returning to my seat I admitted ruefully, "I see your point."

The old tech re-entered the room, pausing by the doorway to place his thumb against yet another disk. As he turned the thumb the indirect lighting in the room got brighter. I wondered if there was anything in the apartment that would work for anyone but him. He came over and placed a tray on the coffee table in front of me.

Drugs or no drugs, the steak and potatoes tasted wonderful.

As I sat there chewing contentedly, the tech sat down across from me and said, "Any questions?"

"Indeed yes," Mary said instantly. "You may begin with your name!"

He laughed. "I call myself Tom Fowler. Doc Tom Fowler."

"You're a Doc?" I said with my mouth full.

"More or less."

"Retired?" I persisted.

"Techs never retire. I am on a reduced work load, because of my age, but I plan to die as I've lived, in the service." This was said with a tone of calm satisfaction.

"How did you know who I was?" I asked.

"Your Doc friend sent me a faxprint of your photo on my videophone. I imagine every Doc on the coast has a pin-up of you by now." He chuckled. "Oh, we've been keeping track of you, never fear. We know about your ocean voyage, your visit to Carmel, everything." He leaned toward me and placed his wrinkled hand on my knee. "But tell me, did you really *have* to steal the Black Maria?" He leaned back and burst out laughing.

Mary was annoyed. "All right, but how did you know we were here in Futuria?"

He was still amused. "We knew as soon as the police

did. You remember that Tin Woodsman of Oz that greeted you when you arrived? Well, there's a closed-circuit television camera in that rascal that connects up with a command post in the basement of Scotland Yard."

Mary was not satisfied. "That explains how the police knew about us, but how did *you* know?"

After a pause, Fowler answered, not without embarrassment. "Well, you see, we tap their phones."

MARY fell asleep in her chair, but I sat up quite late talking to Fowler. I was too sleepy to ask the right questions, so all I found out was that there were some things he was willing to discuss and some things he wasn't.

Among the okay subjects was my "case."

The techs, he told me, had been watching my "case" with interest. They were pleased with my "progress." My progress toward what? Ah, that was something they were *not* willing to discuss. But they were pleased enough with me to help me escape from the police.

I asked, "What if Lestrade pounded on the door this minute and demanded that you hand me over?"

Fowler shrugged. "I'd hand you over. I'm not authorized to provoke a direct confrontation with the local law enforcement agencies." He sighed. "But it would be a pity."

"Listen," I said, "Who has more power, you or Lestrade?"

He frowned. "That's not as easy a question as you might think. I, as a representative of the techs, can call upon a technology Lestrade does not even know exists. Moreover, I know all about Lestrade and he knows nothing about me. In fact the techs know all about Scotland Yard in general, while Scotland Yard has only the vaguest and most inaccurate idea of what we techs are and what we're doing. Finally, we understand human psychology better than anyone in history, while Lestrade is still floundering around with, at best, the naive guesses of Sigmund Freud."

"Well then. . . . " I began.

He held up his hand. "There is another side to the coin. Certainly you must have noticed that we techs are not exactly numerous. Would it surprise you to learn that we constitute less than one tenth of one percent of the world's population? And yet we rule. Make no mistake about that.

Then Beggars Could Ride

We rule. But it is not easy. We cannot afford sudden unplanned moves. We cannot afford to arouse needless hostility. We cannot sacrifice long-term goals to protect individuals, even such promising individuals as you and your charming little friend here." He looked at her fondly. "We have particularly high hopes for Mary. Her I.Q., so far as we are able to determine, falls well into the range of what is called genius. If you two were to mate . . . but I've said too much. You're tired. Let me make up a bed for you."

I was troubled, as I always was by the impressions I got of the techs, but not so troubled that I could not fall asleep and stay asleep until almost noon the following day.

WE had bacon, eggs and toast, Mary, Fowler and I. There was a family feeling in the kitchen as Fowler, dispensing with the services downstairs, prepared our belated breakfast himself. Fowler knew how to prepare simple foods properly, the mark of a truly good cook; the eggs, with butter, in one pan, and the bacon in the other. He held a sharp knife in his hand and whenever the bacon threatened to curl, he notched the contracting portion with his knife so it lay flat and fried evenly.

Mary was as good at eating as he was at cooking. She knew how to eat the soft orange yolk of a fried egg in a single bite, so as not to spill any.

Afterward, as we three sat around the kitchen table dabbing our lips with napkins, Fowler said, "Well, Miss Arthur, my cooking isn't as bad as you thought last night, is it?"

She answered seriously, "Last night I didn't trust you. Today I trust you a little, and that makes a difference in the taste of the food."

"You only trust me a little?" he teased.

"You haven't drugged us. You haven't turned us over to the police," she said. "Yes, I think I can trust you . . . a little. After all, who knows what you might do today?"

I frowned. Mary's paranoia was becoming a pain.

"I hope you trust me enough not to worry if I leave you for a while this afternoon," he said. "I have to go out and see if I can plant a false clue or two for our friend Lestrade, or at least a suitably misleading rumor. Tonight, when that old bloodhound is on the wrong scent, I'll be able to sneak you out of Futuria."

"Why can't we stay here?" she demanded. "At least until things calm down and we can go back to the docks and sign onto some ship?"

Fowler shook his bald head. "That would not be wise. Lestrade is not a fool. He can be led astray for a while, but not forever, and he knows your trail leads through Futuria. What I'm hoping is that we can find some enclave where false identities can be successfully established for you, where you can safely lie low for at least a year."

"A year!" she cried in dismay. "But I'd planned to go to sea this week!"

"Later, Miss Arthur, later."

As Fowler got up to leave, I said, "Are we going to spend the day locked in your apartment while you go about your business?"

He nodded, smiling faintly. "That's right. But all Futurians spend most of their time in their apartments."

"Doing what?" I inquired, feeling a touch of claustrophobia.

"Playing with the Toy."

"The Toy?"

"Come into the front room. I'll show you."

We followed him into the other room where he opened a small chest and produced two helmets, very much like football helmets except that the front extended down to cover the eyes and a cord with a plug at the end came out of the back.

"It's a kind of cable television," he explained. "Except that, for openers, the helmet contains hi-fi stereo headphones and stereoscopic vision. You see, there's a separate small television picture tube in front of each eye. It goes without saying that the color and picture quality on these tubes is so good it's almost impossible to tell you're not looking at real objects. You have a choice of nine hundred channels from stations all over the world; the signal comes in over the telephone lines like an ordinary call. Every tech center and every mim of a possible future has between one and five stations."

I took the helmet in my hands. It was surprisingly light. "But I suppose only you can make it work," I said.

He laughed. "No, no, this thing isn't keyed to my thumb-

Then Beggars Could Ride

print. Anyone can operate it. You see this keyboard?" He indicated a set of disks on the face of the chest arranged like a ten-key adding machine. "You punch up the telephone number of the station you want and the transmission appears—poof—like magic on your screens. If it's a pay station the phone company clocks your time and sends you a bill. If it's a station with advertising, it's free. In addition, you can phone a library computer and get a display of whatever kind of programs you might want, punch up the code number of the exact program, and the library computer will play it off for you and you alone. Once you understand the basic codes you can locate books, too. Any book that's electronically recorded anywhere in the world can be made to appear on your screens, one page at a time, or, working through a computerized cross-reference system, you can get a display of a specific paragraph, even a specific sentence."

I listened in amazement. There had been a videophone terminal in my home which I'd thought was modern, state-of-the-art, but I'd been wrong.

He took back the helmet and turned it over, so I could see the inner surface. "You see these disks on the inner face of the helmet? They're not control disks. They're powerful electromagnets positioned to selectively stimulate different portions of your cerebral cortex. You can turn this part of the system on and off, as you like, but when it's on, and you're watching a movie, magnetic impulses trigger all the right emotional reactions to what you're seeing."

I said thoughtfully, "Can you key into computers?"

"Certainly. And you can get them to solve mathematical problems, if you understand the command codes."

"Let's take an example. Could I key into the advertising computer in Dallas?"

"Easily."

"And could I activate any program I wanted on that computer?"

"Of course."

"And if there was, let us say, a Star Trek spacewar program on that computer, could I key into it and play that game?"

He chuckled. "I've played it myself, many times. It's a masterpiece of game programming, isn't it?"

"A masterpiece," I agreed.

"But when you play on this machine, each phase of the game will be illustrated with a segment of video tape, including several excerpts from the original TV series."

"Really?" I snatched the helmet from him.

"I'll show you the code," he said.

It was an easy code to learn, and all the controls in the Toy were operated from the same ten-key disk keyboard, including the on-off switch.

"Mary," I said delightedly. "There's two helmets here. Let's plug in and have some fun!"

"Oh Bobby," she said, her voice full of disappointment and reproach. "Is that all you can think of to do when you're eloping with someone?"

"One little game? Please?" I pleaded.

"No!" she snapped.

Fowler stood at the door, smiling. He waved to me. I waved back. He thumbed a disk in the wall. The door slid open. He stepped through. The door closed.

He was gone.

I plugged in the jack, keyed in the Dallas computer and the Star Trek game, slipped on the helmet. Yes, I could operate the keyboard by touch alone. Yes, I remembered all the standard codes for the Star Trek game.

I felt Mary tugging at my arm.

"I'll be with you in a minute," I said. "One little game. . . ."

She tugged again and shouted something, but I couldn't hear her very well through the helmet.

Then, abruptly, I seemed to be on the bridge of the Starship Enterprise, watching Mr. Spock raise his eyebrow, and all else was forgotten.

SOMEONE grasped my wrist and gently but firmly removed my hand from the keyboard.

"No," I protested. "Please. One more game. I'm almost ahead." Mr. Spock awaited my decision.

The helmet was lifted off my head. Fowler grinned down at me.

"Are you back already?" I said resentfully.

"What do you mean 'already'?" he demanded. "It's after midnight. You've been playing with the Toy for at least twelve hours."

"No, it can't be that long." I reached for the helmet.

Fowler keyed in the code for "off" and pulled out the

plug jack. "Snap out of it, Newton. You're going to need a clear head. We're moving out."

I looked around, blinking, confused.

As he had said, it was late at night. I could see the dark sky outside the picture window. On one of the super-comfortable chairs nearby Mary lay asleep in a sitting position, a book open in her lap. I felt a pang of guilt. I had neglected her.

Fowler went over and shook her gently by the shoulder, saying softly, "Wake up, Miss Arthur. Wake up."

"Huh? What?" she muttered, startled. Her eyes focused on me. "Thank God you've taken off that stupid helmet and turned back into a human being."

I said, "Don't knock it if you ain't tried it."

She said, "It'll never replace the book." She closed the book she'd been reading with a slam. I caught a glimpse of the title, embossed in gold on its leather binding. "The techman's Manual."

Fowler picked up the book with a frown.

"You didn't want me to read that, did you?" she asked him.

"No," he admitted shortly, replacing it on the shelf.

She laughed at his annoyance.

He opened a battered suitcase and began to take out one article of clothing after another. "Put these on," he said.

I recognized a long-sleeved reddish-plaid shirt, a leather vest, a pair of blue jeans, and a bright red neck scarf. When he produced a pair of boots with spurs, a gunbelt with a six-shooter in the holster, and a ten-gallon hat, I said, "Am I going to be a cowboy?"

"How'd you guess?" said Fowler.

I hated to lose my sailor outfit. It had a kind of sentimental value. But, with a sigh, I began my transformation from seaman to cowpoke.

Mary's new clothes were in the same general style as her old ones, though of a poorer quality. I said, "It's the Old West we're going to, isn't it?"

"The Wild West," said Fowler. "Around 1865. Mary's manners and speech patterns won't be so out of place there."

"What about mine?" I asked.

"You're going to be the strong, silent type," he answered with a touch of irony.

When we were dressed in our western outfits, Fowler checked the halls, then said, "All clear." We hurried to the elevator and went up to the roof.

"Now what?" I demanded.

"Wait a minute." Fowler took out a flashlight and waved its beam skyward. Immediately a soft fluttering sound sorted itself out from the general hum of the city, and down out of the darkness came a small helicopter painted black, without lights or markings. It hovered a moment overhead, then settled gently on the roof near us.

"Quick," whispered Fowler. "Get in."

As we passed under the slowly turning rotors, I gestured toward the engine and asked archly, "Gasoline powered?"

Fowler answered indignantly, "No, methane!"

His tone told me I was being rude to even suggest that the techs might break their own rule against the use of petroleum for fuel, but I thought, *Those techs can't be perfect. Sooner or later I'll catch them in a contradiction.*

We scrambled in and fastened our safety belts. With a momentary lurch, we were airborne.

"Good to see you again, Fowler," said the pilot.

"Good to see you, Mike," said Fowler, leaning forward. With some difficulty, they shook hands. They couldn't have seen each other very well. The only light came from the bright city below and the dim green-glowing instrument panel.

"Did you get off clean?" asked Mike.

"I think so," said Fowler.

Mike nodded soberly, then gestured toward the co-pilot. "Sonny is monitoring the police radio frequencies. What d'ya think, Sonny?"

Sonny gave a thumbs-up signal. "Not a word about the chopper. A half-hour ago they mentioned our passengers here, though."

"What did they say?" Fowler asked.

"Lestrade put out an all-points-bulletin for their arrest and ordered a room-to-room search of all the buildings in this part of Futuria."

"So we got out none too soon," Fowler mused.

"And by the only route left open," Mike added. "Lestrade has men in every exit from the enclave."

I grumbled, "It seems like an awful fuss to make over an elopement."

Then Beggars Could Ride

Mike laughed. "Elopement? Is that what you call it? According to Lestrade it's statutory rape, child molestation, and kidnapping. Any one of those crimes is a capital offense in Sherlock, if it concerns someone of Good Family. And . . . tell the truth, did you actually steal Lestrade's Black Maria?"

"That's right," said Mary, somewhat proudly.

The three techs roared with laughter. When he could speak, Sonny said, "I'd have given anything to see his face."

Mike added, "That's what Lestrade is really after you for, the poor slob." He burst out laughing again.

We had been gaining altitude steadily and now were brushing the lower face of the cloud cover.

Mike pointed downward. "There goes the Santa Monica Mountains." A range of mountains passed quite close below us. We'd left Futuria behind and the cockpit was suddenly much darker. The shimmering, brilliant city had been replaced by a moving blackness broken only by an occasional point of feeble flickering red light.

Fowler said to me, "It's not hard, is it, to tell when you go from a high-energy enclave to a low-energy one?"

"No, I guess not," I said.

After that nobody spoke for a long time; each of us was lost in his own thoughts, listening to the fluttering of the rotors and the rush of the empty night air.

CHAPTER 11

Dawn found me counting on my fingers.

"Today," I murmured. "Tomorrow. The day after tomorrow and the day after that."

Mary rolled over in bed and regarded me with curiosity. "What are you counting?" she asked, rubbing her eyes with her fist like the child she was.

"I'm counting the days until my ship sails."

"Our ship," she corrected me.

I sat on the edge of the bed in my long red flannel underwear and considered my situation. I'd wasted so much precious time. My first day had been wasted in a vain effort to get my all-important papers. (Nobody had yet asked me for them.) My second day had been wasted running away from Mary's parents and the police. And I'd blown the third day playing a simulation game of spacewar. Was that any way to rationally study the local enclaves and wisely select the one where I'd spend the rest of my life?

"Today," I resolved, "will be different."

I stood up, ignoring the morning chill, and padded barefoot over the gritty rugless floor to the window, where I could look down into the street. Directly below, the stagecoach was loading up. With an eye to departure I'd asked the hotel clerk last night about the stagecoach schedule, as we signed the register with the false names that matched the false papers Fowler had given us when he'd let us off a mile from town. The clerk had informed me there was one stage a day; it drove in around sundown and left the following morning.

I had expected the clerk to have some questions of his own. Was it normal for guests to check in after midnight? But the clerk had not shown the slightest curiosity about Mary and me. Perhaps it was considered unwise to be too curious in a town like Ridgepole, where every man wore a pistol on his hip.

"Come back to bed," Mary called in a sleepy voice.

"I'm not going to waste another day."

"Oh, Bobby!" she moaned.

"I'm not Bobby any more. I'm Jonathan Tree. And you're Mrs. Jonathan Tree." Those were the names on our forged papers.

Then Beggars Could Ride

"But those are just false identities."

I answered pedantically, "All identities are false identities."

After a pause she said thoughtfully, "Then are we really married?"

"As far as anyone here knows."

"I'd rather we had some sort of proper ceremony."

"If we asked for one, then everyone would know we weren't married."

Her voice was muffled. She'd buried her head under the pillow. "Beast!" she said.

With a clatter the stagecoach set off down the broad dirt street. I watched it go. "All identities are false identities," I muttered under my breath. The phrase had the ring of some great truth. "It's just that we wear some masks longer than others."

Ridgepole was a small town. The daily stagecoach was its only contact with the outside world. It was a place where one could vanish and never be heard from again, which was no doubt the reason Fowler had chosen it.

There was a cracked mirror above the dresser. I went over and looked at myself in it.

"Hello, Jonathan Tree," I said to me.

"Madman," grumbled Mary.

The man in the mirror did not look at all like a Newton McClintok. He looked like a Jonathan Tree. Newton was a thin, sickly alcoholic. Jonathan was a broad-shouldered, healthy Westerner, a man in, as they put it here, "the prime of his life." The beginnings of a beard and mustache showed around Jonathan's determined jaw. I thought, *Maybe I'll let it grow.*

I could also see Mary in the mirror, still in bed but out from under the pillow again. I thought, *Jonathan has a very young wife.* I chuckled. An old man, but a vigorous one, and a young wife. That probably wasn't too unusual here in Ridgepole.

I took off my long red flannel underwear.

"Are you getting dressed?" Mary asked.

"That's right, dearie." I began humming "Clementine."

"Going out?"

"Yep." I put on the blue jeans with no underwear under them. It would probably be as hot during the day as it had been cold during the night.

"And what do you plan to do?"

"Look for a job," I told her, as I finished dressing.

She didn't seem too happy about the idea, but she made no objection. When she kissed me goodbye, it was not with the enthusiasm she'd shown on earlier occasions.

"See you in a few hours," I said over my shoulder as I went out into the dark hallway. She did not reply.

Whistling, I bounded down the rickety staircase, tipped my ten gallon hat to the desk clerk in passing, and stepped out onto the boardwalk. I turned, thumbs in vest, and looked down the street.

And I saw it for the first time.

A block away the street ended, and beyond lay miles and miles and miles and miles of nothing.

It was not a mim of the Mojave Desert.

It really *was* the Mojave Desert.

I stared at it blankly for a long time before finally turning my back to it and walking in the opposite direction. Ahead of me now was a "T" intersection and a wall of buildings that mercifully hid from me the view that would, no doubt, have been as bleak as the one behind me.

In the center of this wall of buildings I saw a saloon; it bore a gaudy red, yellow and black sign on which, in circus lettering, I read the words "Blind Dick's Bottom Dollar Saloon." I paused on the street corner, frowning. Did I trust myself to work in the middle of all that booze? There would be a risk, but the saloon was far and away the largest building in sight, probably the largest in town. It followed that it would also be the biggest employer.

I waited for a solitary buckboard to rattle past, then stepped into the dirt street. Little clouds of dust puffed out from my boots at every step, depressing evidence of Ridgepole's extreme dryness. It was still early morning, but already the temperature was beginning to rise. I licked my lips and wished for a chapstick.

Or a drink.

I stepped up onto the boardwalk, and pushed through the swinging doors into the dim, relatively cool interior. To my left, running almost the length of the room, I made out a perhaps fifty-foot, dark wood bar fronted by a heavy brass rail. On the wall behind the bar was an equally long mirror, scarred here and there with bullet holes from which radiated webs of fine cracks. The ceiling was high, high enough to allow for a second-floor balcony across the back of the room, reached by a curving staircase on my right. Both ground floor and balcony were filled with battered black circular tables and unoccupied chairs. Next to the stairs a pedal-powered upright player piano awaited the night's entertainments; a wooden chest full of piano rolls stood open beside it.

A lean elderly black looked up from his sweeping to say, "We is closed."

"I don't want a drink." (That was not quite true.) "I want to speak to the manager."

"About what?" He eyed me with suspicion.

"I'm looking for a job."

"You ain't gettin' mine!" He went back to work, pointedly ignoring me.

From the balcony came a grumpy voice. "Someone down there with you, Sam?"

"Yes, sir," answered the black man.

"What's he want?"

"Nuthin'," said Sam.

"I want to talk to you about a job," I called out.

A tap-tap-tap sound broke the silence of the bar. A tall man in a black suit was making his way slowly along the balcony, feeling out his path with a cane. I thought, *So there really is a Blind Dick.* As he reached the head of the stairs, I had an impulse to run up and help him, but he started down at a good pace, without waiting for help from anyone. He evidently had the layout of the saloon memorized.

I met him at the foot of the staircase.

"My name is Dick Collins. Folks call me Blind Dick, for obvious reasons." He held out his hand in my general direction.

I gave him a firm handshake, saying, "I'm Jonathan Tree, sir."

His face, behind a handsome handlebar mustache, was pale and thin. He wore dark glasses. He groped around him, found a chair, and sat down at the nearest table. "Have a seat, stranger," he said.

I sat down across the table from him.

"You're from uptime, aren't you?" he said.

"How did you know?" I said uneasily.

"It's the way you talk, your accent. I'd place you as somewhere in the nineteen-twenties. Right?"

I didn't answer.

He laughed. "Don't want to talk about it, eh? Running away from something, like as not." He leaned forward, his long pale fingers searching for me. "You're on the dodge. Isn't that right?" His fingers found my arm, gave it a little squeeze. "Tell me about it, Mr. Tree. You can trust harmless old Blind Dick."

"I haven't done anything really wrong."

He chuckled. "Of course not. Nobody ever does. Don't worry, Tree. If that *is* your name. I don't mind my employees having a skeleton or two in their closets, especially if I know what the skeleton is, and they know I know." His hand still rested on my arm. I wondered what additional information he was getting about me through the sense of touch. "Come on, pal. What's your crime?"

"Do I have to tell you to get a job?"

"No, no, of course not. I'm just curious, that's all. I like to know my employees. I like to be more than a boss . . . a close friend. Y'understand?" He turned toward Sam. "Ain't that right, Sam?"

"Yes, sir," muttered Sam sullenly. I wondered what Blind Dick had on Sam.

Blind Dick withdrew a small silver box of cigars from his inside coat pocket. "Cigar?" he asked.

"I don't smoke."

"Is that a fact?" He bit off the end of one of the cigars. "Hey, Sam," he called. "Gimme a light!"

Sam came over, pulling some kitchen matches from the breast pocket of his flannel shirt. "Yes, sir, Mister Collins." He held a match steady while Blind Dick sucked the cigar into flame.

"Thanks, Sam," said Collins, exhaling.

Sam went back to work.

"Drink?" asked Collins, turning to me again.

"No thanks."

"What's this? You don't smoke and you don't drink? What are you? Some kind of Holy Roller?"

"No, sir."

"A teetotaler?"

"Not exactly. It's only that if I take one drink, it may lead to two, and then—"

He snatched back his hand. "Hold it! Hold it! I can see you now. I can see you clear as day."

"You can see me?" I was amazed.

"Yeah! You've got blue veins showing in your nose and cheeks. Right?"

"No, that's not so!"

"And you got red, watery eyes."

"No!"

He leaned back in his chair and said, "Ain't that right, Sam? Ain't he got red watery eyes?"

"That's right, sir." Sam had an evil grin.

"Y'see?" gloated the blind man. "Think you can fool me? Think you can take advantage of my infirmity? You got another guess comin', mister. I don't mind drunks in this saloon. I love 'um! But only on the customer's side of the bar!"

"You're making a mistake—" I began desperately.

"Move on, wino," he growled. "Get out of my saloon."

"But—"

"Move!" he shouted. His pale features were turning red with fury.

I pushed back my chair and got up.

As I was going out through the swinging doors I heard Collins bellow, "Whiskey, Sam!"

"Yes, sir, Mistah Collins," the black man answered with satisfaction.

My first job interview had left something to be desired. My second interview, at the blacksmith's shop, had been less traumatic but no more successful. My third try was the barbershop.

The barber, a Mr. Morris Benton, was a genial middle-aged man in shirtsleeves, bow tie, and bright red suspenders. He was polite and sympathetic, though he went right on shaving a heavyset fellow in the barber chair all during the interview. "I'm sorry," said Benton. "If you're not a graduate of a barber's school, I can't use you."

I said glumly, "I don't know if there's anything I can do that's in demand in this town."

"Well," said Morris, with a flourish of the razor, "what did you used to do?"

"Selling, I guess you'd call it.'

The man in the barber chair broke in. "Selling you say?"

"That's right." I was about to explain that actually I'd been in advertising.

"I can use a good salesman," said the man in the chair.

"Wait until I'm finished here and I'll take you over to my store."

"Anything you say, sir!"

"Dutton's the name," said the man.

"I'm Jonathan Tree." He reached out from under the barber's sheet and shook my hand.

Dutton was something of a dandy. In spite of the temperature, which was now entering the sweat-and-pant range, he insisted on wearing a frock coat, vest, silk neck scarf and high black derby hat.

"I own the general store," he explained as we left the barbershop. "I really need another fellow around, someone mature, trustworthy." He looked me over. "You might be exactly the man I want."

The store was across the street from the saloon, barbershop, and blacksmith's, and down about a block. The tall sans-serif lettering on the sign announced "Dutton's Dry Goods Emporium." The rectangular front of the store, almost a full story taller than the actual roof, was impressively ornate, all of painted iron, with vaguely Corinthian columns separating the display windows from the central door, and twisting stylized floral designs in cast iron filling up every available space.

Jutting out over the boardwalk was a permanent awning made of corrugated galvanized iron, supported at the curb by iron pipes. We stood in the welcome shade of this awning while Dutton searched through his many pockets for his key, finally found it with a cry of delight, and unlocked the front door. As the door opened a tiny bell attached to it gave a tinkle.

"You see?" he said as he closed the door behind us. "I have to lock up every time I go out. There's no telling how many customers I lose that way. If there were two of us ... well, you can see the advantages."

"Indeed I can."

"I had a young fellow here a few months ago."

"Oh? What happened to him?"

"He moved on. Ridgepole wasn't exciting enough for him, I guess."

The store was relatively cool and had a fascinating smell. There were spices and the aroma of freshly ground coffee in the dim quiet air; candy, tobacco, and mothballs also competed for dominance; but the smell that finally ruled over all was that of blackstrap molasses.

Then Beggars Could Ride

"Let me show you around," he said.

We moved from counter to counter as he proudly recited a seemingly endless list of the products available. "We have canned fruits and vegetables, tea, sugar, dried fruits and chocolates. We have knives, axes, rifles, pistols, ammunition, kitchen utensils, agricultural implements, horse collars and nails. We have shoes and boots for both sexes and all ages. We have pins and needles, threads, ribbons and even some fine treadle sewing machines. We have jewelry, clocks and watches. We have organs—if you're a religious man—and a fine upright piano for only ninety-eight dollars. We have hats; everything from Victoria bonnets to derbys. We have clothing for ladies and gentlemen, as well as for the working class. And we have a modest selection of books . . . nothing spicy, you understand." He winked at me. "And should you wish to write a letter, here we have paper, pen and envelopes, and when it's time to mail it, I'm the postmaster and this store's the post office."

"It's a perfect mim," I said in genuine awe.

Dutton beamed. "And in daily use, I'll have you know. The authenticity of Ridgepole is in no small measure due to the efforts of Dutton's Dry Goods Emporium. There's nothing plastic here, nothing uptime. Every item is perfectly in period. I'm glad to see you have a feeling for a good mim. That young man I was telling you about . . . he didn't care a fig for period. But he was better than nothing." He was looking at me hopefully, and I realized with surprise that here, for once, my labor was being offered in a seller's market.

When I didn't instantly accept his offer, he said, "Are you married?"

"Yes."

"I'm a single man myself, but I like a married man . . . as an employee, that is. A married man's more settled. A married man's not going to up and run off to Futuria looking for cheap thrills." I gathered this was what the "young man" had done. "I'll tell you what I'll do. Your missis would like a nice home, I'm sure."

"I suppose so."

"What if I was to provide, as part of your wages, a fine little four-room cottage close by here?"

"Why, that would be wonderful," I said.

"Not so fast. Don't you want to look at the house? Don't you want to know your salary?" He quoted the salary. It was low, but then, so were the prices of everything I'd seen in the store.

"And as for the house," I said, "I hope you don't mind if I go and get the wife. She should be the one to decide about that."

"Right you are!"

We went together to the hotel and found Mary in the dining room having lunch. (It was now somewhat after noon.) I was very enthusiastic, and so was Dutton. Mary was cool to the idea at first, but before dessert was served she'd been largely won over.

As we three trooped down the baking street toward our new home, she seemed even more excited and curious than I was. The surprising thing was that the house actually was a beautiful little place, a one-story wood frame house freshly painted white with a brown shingle roof, in good repair and sparsely but tastefully furnished.

Dutton showed off the interior of the house with the same pride he'd displayed in showing off his store, finishing by saying, "Now I'll leave you married folk to settle in and get comfortable. Will I see you at the store tomorrow, Mr. Tree, at seven?"

The time seemed a little early, but I said, "Yes, sir, Mr. Dutton."

As he turned to go, Mary added, "And thank you, Mr. Dutton. You don't know how much this means to us."

"Think nothing of it," he chuckled, pushing open the screen door.

When he had gone, Mary and I went from room to room, oohing and ahing at everything all over again.

"Do you think we'll be happy here?" I whispered, some time later.

"For a while," she said.

"A while?"

"Until we can go to sea together."

So she was still dreaming of the sea. I had tried the sea and found it wanting. As I looked around at the flowery wallpaper, the massive dresser, and the pitcher and basin on it, I realized that I would be content—or so it seemed to me at that moment—to spend the rest of my life here in

Then Beggars Could Ride

Ridgepole, working at the store during the day and spending the nights with "Mrs. Tree." The long restless search for utopia had ended.

Toward evening Mary and I walked slowly back to the hotel to pick up our suitcase, hand in hand, saying nothing. Occasionally I glanced at her, wondering if she could possibly be as happy as I was, and every time I looked she was smiling.

We got our suitcase and checked out.

"Taking the stage?" asked the clerk as he hung up our key.

"The stage?" I said, startled.

"Sure. The stage just came in a few minutes ago," he explained. "I wanted to be sure you knew it wouldn't be leaving until tomorrow morning."

"We know about that," said Mary.

"We're not going anywhere," I said, grinning. "We're going to settle down right here in Ridgepole."

"In that case," said the clerk, "Welcome, neighbor."

He reached across the counter and shook my hand. It was a sincere, friendly handshake.

I was still grinning as Mary and I stepped out onto the boardwalk, into the ruddy glow of sunset.

Then I noticed the poster nailed to the wall of the hotel. "Have you seen this girl?" was printed in bold headlines. The picture was a photograph of Mary.

Mary had seen it the same moment as I had. She whispered, "Oh no." I quickly scanned the fine print. There was, it said, a reward for information leading to her recovery.

And my arrest.

Farther down the street two men were busy nailing up more posters exactly like it. They both wore some sort of star on their vests.

"They must have come in on the stagecoach," I said softly.

Mary's voice was angry. "Jonathan, can you ride?"

"Ride what?" I answered stupidly.

"A horse! What do you think? A kiddie car?"

"No. No, I never had any occasion to learn."

"Then there's only one thing to do," she muttered with disgust.

"And what is that?"

"Steal a buckboard."

RIDGEPOLE was far behind us when the gibbous moon appeared over the crest of the distant mountains, casting a spectral glow over the gently rolling dessert. Only then did Mary, who drove the team of horses with appalling skill, allow them to slow from a gallop to a trot. For a long time the only sound was the rattle and creak of the buckboard, then I said, "Where can we go? If your picture is way out here in Ridgepole, it must be everywhere."

For once, it seemed, Mary had no smart answer.

She didn't even weep, which was too bad, because it meant I couldn't weep myself without losing face.

CHAPTER 12

I awoke smelling the sea and sat up, stretching my cramped body. The buckboard had halted; the horses were munching grass. Mary sat beside me on the hard buckboard seat, her head drooping with weariness. I looked around me.

At the zenith the sky was growing rapidly brighter. To my right and to my left the silhouettes of tall palm trees were becoming visible. Ahead of me lay a body of water. It was too calm to be the sea; mirror-smooth and, like a mirror, reflecting a few distant points of flickering light.

Millions of birds were singing, and some of them glided across the face of the water, catching the fish that occasionally leaped up out of the depths. It was a lake, I decided. And not a very large one.

"Where are we?" I asked in a low voice.

She gestured toward the points of light on the other side of the lake. "That's the City of Isis. We're on its outer boundary."

"The City of Isis?"

"It's a mim of first century A.D. Egyptian Alexandria. The patron gods of Alexandria are the Great Father Osiris-Serapis and the Great Mother Isis. I've never been here before, but Herbert has told me about it."

I shrugged. "One city is the same as another, as far as we're concerned. Everyone will know your face here, too."

"It doesn't matter," she said.

"What do you mean?"

"In Egypt a woman can keep her face covered with a veil. It's a custom that probably originated with the ancient nuns of Isis and was later adopted by the Moslems, just as the early Christians adopted the custom of having monasteries and nunneries from the pagan worshippers of Isis and Osiris-Serapis." She had taken a white silk scarf from the suitcase and tied it around her face, and now wrapped around her slender body a threadbare horse blanket we'd found in the buckboard.

"What about me?" I asked.

"There's another blanket in the wagon. You lie under it and try to look as much as possible like a sack of flour. Then we'll go into town and—"

"What's the use, Mary? There's no place we can hide once we get there."

"Yes, there is. In the Jewish quarter there is a sect of primitive Christians. They give sanctuary to all, no questions asked."

"Even wanted criminals?"

"Especially wanted criminals. Herbert says they believe that it's the worst sinners who are potentially the best Christians."

I sighed. "It's no use, Mary. You're grasping at straws. Don't you see? If you went on without me and gave yourself up, nothing much would happen to you. It's me they're really out to nail to the wall. You could be safe at home tonight, in your own bed with your own ship pictures and your own ship model, with your parents to buy you anything your heart desires, and servants to tend to your every need."

She said curtly, "If I wanted that, I wouldn't be here."

"Go back, Mary. Go back before your luck runs out."

"And then what would you do, eh? You can't drive a team of horses, you can't speak Greek or Latin—and those are the main languages spoken in Isis—and you're not too bright all around. Without me, Lestrade would have you in his nets in a wink of the eye. Besides, it's I who got you into all this. It's a matter of honor that I should get you out again. I can see you now, blundering into some trap in your usual fashion. You're such a helpless creature. You can't do anything at all on your own!"

I glanced toward the lake where the skyline of Isis could be clearly seen in reflection. "I can swim," I said hopefully. "I was captain of my swimming team in college."

"Is that so? And what earthly use is that? Do you expect to spend the rest of your life in the lake like some kind of fish?"

"I suppose not," I said gloomily.

She grasped my shoulders with her delicate little hands and said fiercely, "Stiff upper lip, old chum. We're not splitting apart for anything, and that's final. You're my husband, and I shan't give you up for anything. I love you, you silly thing. Don't you understand that? I love you!"

She kissed me roughly, angrily on the lips, through her silk scarf.

Then Beggars Could Ride

I kissed her back, knowing that it meant I was giving in to her.

Then I crawled under the seat with the blanket wrapped around me, Mary clucked her tongue and gave the reins a shake, and the buckboard was on the move again.

After a moment I said softly, "But why this particular city?"

She answered crisply, "I explained all that. And besides, Isis is a seaport. We can ship out from here."

As we clupped along Mary explained how the City of Isis had been built at San Clemente, with the Temple of Osiris-Serapis in his aspect of God of the Underworld constructed exactly on the site of the former home of Richard Nixon, an obscure president of the Sinister Seventies. The techs had done a drastic job of remodeling the terrain, digging out the lake (called Lake Mariotis) and using the dirt to make a one-for-one scale model of the island of Pharos in the harbor. On this island they built an exact copy, as nearly as archeological science permitted, of the original Great Lighthouse of Alexandria, over four hundred feet tall.

From time to time she would cease her muttered travelog and I would hear her exchange greetings with people she passed on the road, sometimes in Latin, sometimes in Greek. Her accent must have been pretty good, because everyone accepted her without question as one of the natives. I reflected that Mary might be one of the few young ladies in her private school to find practical use for a classical education.

Although I didn't dare peek out, I knew by the sound of the wheels when we had ceased to roll on dirt roads and started to roll on paving-stones. All around were the noises of the other people and animals in the street, the murmur of foreign tongues, and the strong smell of animal dung and rancid olive oil. (The olive oil was used in the city's lamps.)

The temperature was rising, particularly under my heavy horse-blanket, and it was not the dry heat of the dessert, but the sticky humid heat of the seaside. I was bathed in sweat, but dared not move, dared not raise the blanket for a single breath of fresh air.

From time to time Mary would rein up and ask directions, and I could tell from the steadily increasing crowd noise that we must be making our way into the very heart of the city. Finally she leaned close to me and whispered, "We're entering the Jewish Quarter." As we moved on I could tell that the babble had changed from Greek and Latin to some sort of Hebrew. (I suppose it must have been Aramaic.)

Still we stopped again and again, but now for longer periods, as Mary would climb down from the buckboard and carry on long conversations in whispers with various apprehensive strangers in Greek. (It seemed that most of the Jews here spoke at least two languages.)

At last someone—a man with a gruff friendly voice—got into the buckboard with her, and we began to move along at a brisker pace. This time, when we stopped, Mary said, "Quick, Jonathan. All's clear. Come on." She shook me by the shoulder as if to awaken me.

I struggled into a sitting position and found myself blinded by sunlight.

"Get out of the wagon," she urged. "Someone may discover us at any moment."

"I can't see," I protested.

At this two strong pairs of hands dragged me roughly out of the wagon. There were several men around me, muttering nervously in Greek. Before I could catch my balance I was propelled across a stretch of paving stones and into a shadowy doorway where my eyes began to function. I saw a blur of brown, bearded, worried-looking faces and, out in the blazing sunlight, someone (not Mary) riding off in the buckboard.

Then, still not able to clearly make out where I was going, I was hurried through a dark narrow passageway and down a flight of stone stairs. Mary and the gruff-voiced stranger exchanged a few remarks in Greek, then he and his friends went up the stairs and out through the heavy door, slamming it and locking it.

"Don't move yet," Mary warned. "There are jars of wine all around us. You don't want to knock one over."

"Are they gone? Those men?"

"That's right. We're alone."

"Who were they?"

Her voice was triumphant. "Christians! I told you they'd take us in."

There was a little light coming into the room from the cracks around the edge of the door, and as my eyes became

Then Beggars Could Ride

accustomed to the dimness, Mary's face materialized out of the gloom, proud, exhilarated, and gleeful.

WE were in a wine cellar.

I could quite clearly see the rows of jars or bottles (Mary called them *amphorae*) that stood in wooden racks here in the cool darkness. The jars were tall, two-handled, earthenware things, narrow at the neck and fat at the belly, of several measured sizes. Though they were all more or less alike, all were somewhat irregular in shape. There was not enough light to determine their colors.

It was not uncomfortable in the cellar, certainly more comfortable than it had been outside, though it did seem a bit damp. Mary and I found a heap of straw in a corner away from the stairs and sat down. She laid her head on my shoulder and sighed. I leaned back against the rough stone wall.

I said, "You took some awful chances, talking to strangers like that."

"What else could I do?"

"How did you know they wouldn't turn you over to the police?"

"I only talked to Jews. They know what it is to be hunted. There are Greeks and Jews and native Egyptians and a few Romans in the city, and each dresses in a different way. The Greeks and Romans are almost all clean-shaven, and the Romans, if they're full citizens, wear togas. The Jews wear beards and have a blue border on their robes."

"It sounds like a good mim."

"It's a *beautiful* mim! As I rode through the streets I could have sworn Herbert's time machine had really worked."

"How long are we going to stay in this cellar?"

"Don't worry, Johnny. The leader of the Christians will be here soon to talk to us. Then I'm sure they'll help us get the right kind of clothing and some place to live. What I'm actually hoping for is that they'll help us find a ship."

We talked a while longer, there in the quiet shadows, and even laughed a few times, though not very loud. Finally I asked, "Who is this leader of the Christians?"

"The Apostle Mark," she said.

Before I had time to comment on this surprising revelation, the door opened and two men in tunic, cloak and sandals stood at the head of the stairs, squinting in at us. A woman somewhere out of sight said something to them in Greek and they started down. The men were bearded, brown, weathered, and muscular. In the light from the open doorway, I could see that both were in their thirties or forties, with black hair and eyes.

Mary sprang to her feet and went forward to kneel before them as they reached the bottom of the stairs, kissing the ring of first one then the other. I walked behind her, but could not bring myself to do the kneeling and ring-kissing.

The door closed and again we were in near-total darkness.

They spoke to her in Greek, and she answered. One of the men did most of the talking, in a gentle, almost playful voice. Mary turned to me and said, "Jonathan. I want you to meet the Apostle Mark, founder of the Alexandrian Christian Church and author of one of the Gospels." She seemed to expect me to finally kneel, but I couldn't. Instead I reached out my right hand for a handshake.

Mark responded by grasping my wrist, and I found myself shaking hands with him hand-to-wrist, Roman style. He did not seem in the least offended by my failure to show proper respect, though Mary frowned at me. (Or I think she frowned. I could not see her face too clearly.)

He spoke to me earnestly in Greek and Mary translated. "He wants you to meet his second-in-command, Annianus, first Bishop of this city, who will rule the church here when Mark's work takes him elsewhere."

I shook hands, Roman-style again, with the other man.

Annianus said something softly. Mary translated, "He says, may Yahweh guide you."

I said, "Tell them we'll need the guidance of Yahweh, all right, and also some clothes suitable to this enclave, and a place to stay until we can find a ship out of here."

She forwarded my message. The men nodded. Yes, they would provide clothing. Yes, they would provide a hiding place. Yes, they would help us find a ship out, if that was what we wanted. Many were the Christians who came and went without the knowledge of the authorities.

Then Beggars Could Ride

But was a ship what we really wanted? Would we, by fleeing, find some place that was better than this? (She'd told him of my search for utopia.)

Mark seated himself on the steps.

He suggested that the search for utopia on Earth was doomed to failure. No way of life formed by imperfect Man could be perfect. Perfection was a quality, not of men, but of God. If it was perfection I was seeking, then I should turn to the government of God, and God was to be found as much in one place as in another. God was never too far away to hear me if I called on Him, even in this wine cellar, even at this exact moment.

This sermonette, translated by Mary, made me uncomfortable. These people were taking serious risks for us. How could we then argue with their religious ideas? I said, "Mary, tell Mark I'll give that serious consideration."

She translated.

Mark asked me to consider those things that made men unhappy. What were they? First of all, insecurity. An Alexandrian Christian had no cause for insecurity. The Christians held all money and property in common. A Christian knew that in time of trouble, he could depend on his brothers and sisters in Christ to help him.

Was there another cause for unhappiness? War! The Christians had no part in war. Theirs was a church of the Sixth Commandment, *Thou shalt not kill*. Many a Christian had died rather than become a killer, for all men must die but no man really must kill.

Yet another cause for unhappiness? A lack of meaning and purpose! But there was meaning and purpose in a Christian's life. Each Christian had a task. The Church was the body of Jesus on Earth until the time He returned to rule in person. Each Christian was a hand, a leg, an eye, an ear or a mouth of that body.

And what about loneliness? How could anyone be lonely, surrounded by brothers and sisters in Christ? How could anyone be lonely when the Lord himself was always near, could always be spoken to in prayer?

I must admit I was moved by this argument, even though it must have lost something in translation, but I could not get out of my mind the image of the church Marge had gone to in Chaplin. There, in that church, there had been theatrical productions, political action groups, philosophical discussions, dances, wild parties . . .

but there'd been precious little of Jesus and the name of Yahweh was never mentioned. There'd been no communal ownership of property. Each parishioner had competed with every other parishioner in the ostentatious display of personal wealth. And as for war, the church had held services honoring soldiers who died in war. And as for meaning and purpose, the church itself had been a seeker, not a finder, of meaning, never willing to plainly say, "This is right. That is wrong." And loneliness? I'd never seen a better illustration of the old sociological expression, "The Lonely Crowd."

Through Mary, I tried to explain this.

Mark listened thoughtfully, then spoke to Mary with a heavy sadness in his voice.

Mary translated, "Uptime the Christian Church has strayed far from its origins. It wanders, rootless, lost, seduced by worldliness. The uptime church has no salvation to give, but must itself seek salvation."

"Where? How?" I demanded.

Mary translated the answer with a frown.

Mark had touched his fellow Christian, Bishop Annianus, on the elbow and said softly, "They must do a mim of us."

I HAD been afraid that my refusal to become a convert would lead to the Christians refusing us help, but such was not the case. I was provided with a tunic of white linen, a wool cloak, and some leather sandals that strapped up around the ankles. Though I was not a Jew, the border of the cloak contained the blue fringe that only Jews were supposed to wear. Mary informed me that this detail had bothered the Christians' consciences a little, but they had gone along with it because it might make the difference between life and death for me.

Mary's costume consisted of a long pale blue linen shirt next to the skin, an ankle-length dress over that, and finally a cloak with a cowl and a white veil. The veil effectively covered her face, and the cowl her long blond hair, while the voluminous hanging folds of the dress and shirt disguised her figure so well I hardly recognized her.

"That will fool anyone," I told her as she admired herself in the mirror in the bedroom of the same house where we'd been hiding in the wine cellar.

"Not anyone," she corrected me. "My parents would

know me, I think. And so would Lestrade. Remember, Lestrade has been a friend of our family since I was a baby."

"We're not likely to meet up with either Lestrade or your parents here," I said.

"I certainly hope you're right."

A woman came to the door of the bedroom and spoke to us in Greek, then departed.

"What did she say, Mary?" I asked.

"She said it's time we came to supper." Mary turned toward the door. "But before we go in, I should give you a lesson in Greek."

"Not now!"

"It won't hurt you to learn just one little phrase."

"Oh, all right."

"Repeat after me: *Mah . . . Lee . . . Stah.*"

"*Mah . . . Lee . . . Stah.*"

"Now quicker, and put the accent on the first syllable."

"*Mahleestah!*"

"Oh, that was capital!"

"What did I say?"

"You said yes."

"Fine. Now teach me how to say no."

"You shan't be needing that as yet," she said playfully, leading me into the hall.

The front part of the house, we found, was a large room that may once have been some sort of restaurant. At any rate it now held three rows of long heavy tables, four tables to a row, with couches around each one on three sides. A fairly large group of men and women already reclined on the couches, the men on one side of the room and the women on the other.

When I saw that the men and women would be separated, I said, "Wait a minute. How will I be able to talk to anyone without you to translate? I don't know any Greek."

She answered teasingly, "You know *mahleestah*. That should be enough." And with that she left me and went to the other side of the room.

Some of the men gestured toward me. I thought I recognized them as the ones who'd dragged me out of the buckboard earlier in the day and went over to them. With eloquent pantomime they invited me to share their table.

"*Mahleestah,*" I said.

They laughed with delight and made room, jabbering at me a torrent of friendly jibberish. Then, abruptly, the room fell silent. Everyone rose from a reclining to a kneeling position and tilted back their heads. Some closed their eyes and some extended their arms. I contented myself with kneeling and tilting back my head.

The Apostle Mark stood up and began to speak in an impressive sonorous monotone. He was, I guessed, saying grace. At any rate, when he finished the eating began. The food was simple and rough, but everything was fresh. It was all eaten with the fingers except for the soup, for which we had large wooden spoons. I was so hungry that whenever something was offered to me, I was able to say *mahleestah* with perfect sincerity.

When the eating was done the singing began.

The rhythm was slow and regular, and the vocal timbre harsh and nasal. A number of musical scales were used that were by no means the major and minor I was used to; it was all monophonic, with no suggestion of harmony or counterpoint, yet it was curiously moving, even on first hearing.

Bishop Annianus led off, singing what one might call the solo while everyone listened intently, then all joined in on the chorus. The tune of the chorus was so simple, and the words so repetitious, that I soon found myself singing along, in spite of both the language barrier and the barrier of an unfamiliar musical style. My table mates were delighted with my performance. Between hymns they encouraged me with somewhat undignified slaps on the back and punches in the arm.

I was startled to find that I was genuinely enjoying myself. I'd never realized that religion could be fun.

After many a fine hymn, Bishop Annianus sat down and Apostle Mark stood up, raising his hands for silence. He then made a short speech which was greeted with a murmur of approval and a general nodding of heads.

He turned toward the women's side of the room and beckoned. To my surprise, Mary stood up and walked toward him. And then he turned toward the men's side of the room and beckoned toward me!

My table mates helped me to my feet and propelled me in the direction of the central table where the Apostle waited, smiling.

Then Beggars Could Ride

When I was close enough to her, I whispered to Mary, "What's happening?"

She whispered back, "You and I are getting married."

I protested, "No, no, I can't!"

"Yes, you can," she said firmly. "Just remember, whenever the Apostle asks you a question, you answer *mahleestah*!"

CHAPTER 13

It had been a good night. Mary had wanted to be married with a "proper ceremony," and what could be more proper than a ceremony performed by Saint Mark himself? (Or a reasonable facsimile.) It seemed to me now that anything Mary wanted she would get, no matter how great the opposition, no matter how far-fetched the desire. I had at first thought her idea of going to sea was a naive girlish fantasy, a daydream inspired by an old folksong, but after seeing her in action I'd changed my mind.

As we retired to the blankets on the straw in the corner of the wine cellar, she behaved that night with a shameless, delighted abandon I had never known before and have never known since. This was the emotional volcano that slumbered beneath the surface of Victorianism, all the more violent for its long containment under a calm, utterly respectable exterior. It was interesting to compare, as I lay there with Mary sleeping in my arms, the Victorian Age with the Roaring Twenties: the Victorians, outwardly the most repressed people in history, inwardly possessed an unequaled passion, genius and love of life; the jazz babies of the twenties outwardly liberated from all semblance of restraint but inwardly obsessed with a vast, gray, omnivorous boredom.

Her eyes fluttered open.

"What time is it?" she asked, after yawning.

"There's no way of knowing down here, but it must be sometime in the morning. There's light coming in around the door."

"When is your ship leaving?"

"You mean *The Flying Dutchman*? Tomorrow morning, probably around dawn. We might as well forget about the *Dutchman*."

She kissed me, then said softly, "I don't want to forget about the *Dutchman*."

"We'll never be able to reach it. Lestrade will have every road into the harbor blocked."

"Then we shan't go by road. We'll go by sea. Sherlock is only a little way north of here, up the coast. We can rent a small boat and sail up. Then, when it's night and foggy, we can row in very quietly and climb on board the *Dutchman*, and Lestrade will never be the wiser."

Then Beggars Could Ride

I shook my head dubiously. "Wouldn't it be better to lie low for a while, like the techs advised us? At least until Lestrade gives up on us."

"No, Johnny dear. Certainly not. You don't know Lestrade as I do. He's not a brilliant man, but he has the determination of a British bulldog. He never quite gives up on a case, even when it's been dormant for years. And he'll be more stubborn than usual when he has a personal interest, as he does with us. We'll not be safe until we are completely outside his jurisdiction, in South America or at least Mexico or . . ." she gave me another kiss, this time on the tip of the nose ". . . at sea, beyond the twelve-mile limit."

"It sounds unnecessarily dangerous," I grumbled.

"You said you were a good swimmer."

"That's not the point."

"What's really dangerous is to hang around too long in Mister MacGregor's garden, if you happen to be a rabbit. So get up, slackabed. We've things to do."

We dressed and went upstairs. It was midmorning.

In the kitchen a woman explained that we were way too late for breakfast. Mary translated, "She says the congregation is in the habit of getting up before dawn and going to the cemetery to sing hymns until the sun comes up."

"The cemetery?"

"That's right. So their brothers and sisters who are asleep with Christ can enjoy the music. Afterward they come back here for a communal breakfast, then go about their business. We've missed a lot by sleeping in, as you can see."

All the same the woman relented and set out bread, cheese and goat's milk, which Mary and I devoured.

Mary told the woman we were going down to the waterfront, and that if we did not return they were not to worry, as that only meant we'd moved on.

As we went down the hallway toward the doorway through which we'd originally, somewhat unceremoniously, entered, I said, "You didn't tell her much. Don't you trust her? I mean, these people are real Christians."

Her answer was ironic. "So was Judas Iscariot."

THE words "Have you seen this girl?" were translated into Latin and Greek and, here and there, even into

Egyptian hieroglyphics. Mary's picture, too, had been translated, from a formal Victorian photograph to a line drawing in the realistic but big-eyed Greco-Roman style. Unfortunately the drawing retained the likeness.

The posters stared out at us accusingly from one wall after another as we pushed our way through the crowded streets toward the waterfront. All the same, nobody gave us a second glance. The veil and native costume were, it seemed, disguise enough for Mary and, though my face was exposed, there had been only descriptions of me so far, not pictures.

The city was, to an extraordinary degree, made of stone. Public buildings and private residences alike were mostly marble, and many of the roofs were of red tile. The streets, though crowded and chaotic, were broad and straight and invariably intersected at right angles. It was a triumph of city planning. The architecture looked so modern it was hard to believe it was a true mim, what with its public drinking fountains, shops with awnings, statues, and many-storied buildings. Mary assured me that its modern appearance was due simply to the practice of modern architects of copying classical styles.

The crowd was dressed in a great variety of costumes, though the dominant style was Greek. Here and there I saw some men who wore nothing at all and acted as if this were perfectly normal, as it must have been since nobody paid the slightest attention to them. Mary explained that these nude men were slaves. The only passersby that she took note of were the occasional Roman Legionaries who made their way sullenly through the throng in twos and fours, wearing tunics and cloaks of various colors, iron helmets and breastplates, dagger and shortsword sheathed, leather sandals (almost half-boots) strapped up the ankle, and carrying tall rectangular shields. These soldiers Mary tried to steer us away from as much as possible.

At one point I asked her, "Why Roman soldiers?"

She seemed surprised by my ignorance. "Didn't you know? During the first century A.D. Alexandria was under Roman domination. I mean, what wasn't?"

At the very center of the city two streets, both so wide they were almost fairways, intersected, and here we passed a massive windowless building that, she informed me, was a mim of the tomb of Alexander the Great, but, she added, this tomb was more an informed guess than a true mim. Nobody knew what the original actually looked like.

We passed temples dedicated to a variety of pagan gods, all looking markedly Greek, though the majority were of Egyptian origin. It was not until we had reached a wide public square that fronted on the water on one side that we found something really Egyptian; two towering inscribed obelisks of pink marble. These, Mary whispered, were certainly authentic, since the originals were preserved to this day in London and New York. We passed between them and came to the water's edge.

The sunlight danced in brilliant flaming patterns on the surface; small waves lapped at the brick quays. At intervals the face of the quays was broken by huge cubes of porous, light-yellow travertine limestone, each with a large circular hole through it. To these cubes were moored a number of sumptuously carved and painted biremes, masts removed and oars stacked aft on high T-shaped racks.

I whispered, "I hope you don't think you can steal one of those."

"No," she said wistfully. "They take too big a crew." The disappointment in her voice indicated she had given the idea some consideration before rejecting it.

Directly in front of us was the island of Pharos, with its immense lighthouse on one end. Between us and the island a multitude of vessels rode at anchor; a few, some under sail and some under oar, were arriving or leaving, and we could hear the distant thump of the oarmaster's drum and the singing of the rowers.

To our left and some distance away a long narrow landbridge connected the island with the mainland, and along this landbridge the moored seacraft were most thickly clustered. Some of the ships were out-of-period, but most were the square-rigged Roman grain ships characteristic of the first century, many going so far as to carry the carved figure of a swan facing to the rear. There were biremes too, and triremes that under oar looked so much like some sort of giant water-walking bugs. And there were the feluccas, with their sweeping lateen sails bright-patterned as butterfly wings.

"Come along." Mary whispered, and we walked with no undue haste toward the landbridge.

As we approached it, I could see a great many small

craft, some no bigger than rowboats but, unlike the rowboats I was used to, pointed on both ends and steered by a tiller oar instead of a rudder; there was indeed no difference between the front and rear of these boats. Some of the smallest of them had masts, though they were shallow draft and had no centerboards, and thus would require some fancy seamanship to avoid capsizing in any decent wind. It was one of these that Mary pointed to as she said, "That should do nicely."

We walked out along the landbridge, crossing a span of ordinary bridge to reach it. The landbridge stretched out ahead of us like a somewhat cluttered highway; cluttered with fishermen selling their catch, and with their customers. As we worked our way along, Mary engaged first one, then another fisherman in conversation. I did not need to speak Greek to understand what was meant when she offered a man a handful of the coins she had exchanged with the Christians for her dollars, and the man pushed the money away.

She did not speak to me until we'd reached the center of the landbridge, then I asked, "What's wrong?"

"They don't trust me to bring back the boat, or they think a woman on board would bring them bad luck, or they think I'm playing some kind of joke. Each has a different excuse." She was flushed and angry. "Even when I say I'm acting on your behalf, they won't pay any attention."

"Those boats are, I guess, their only means of making a living," I mused.

"I know! I understand their problems! And they'd get their boat back, of course, when we were done with it. The police would recover it for them. But they don't understand our problem, and if we explained it, they'd turn us in."

"So you're going to steal one of the boats?"

"That's right," she said grimly.

"I don't think the Christians would approve of—"

"Quiet! I'm thinking!"

I stood silently beside her as she glanced first this way, then that, muttering to herself, shading her eyes with her hand. At last she said, "It looks as if they have a gate on the landward side of the bridge that they lock up at night. If we were on the mainland side of that gate, it wouldn't be easy to get through." She turned to face the island. "There's no gate on the island end."

"So we hide on the island and wait for darkness," I concluded.

She looked at me, her eyes glittering from the narrow space between the edge of her cowl and the top of her veil. "You're learning!" she said approvingly.

We walked the rest of the way to the island without any more attempts to bargain. As Mary might have put it, they'd had their chance.

The island, when we reached it, proved to be a poor place to hide. It was long and narrow and had no vegetation; the sea wind, seasoned with salt spray, was no friend to green growing things. Nor were there any caves, or sheltering rock formations; on the landward side there was a smooth but narrow beach, and on the seaward side a sheer rock cliff, pounded by heavy surf.

The immense lighthouse, more impressive than ever up close, was the only major structure on the island. There were two small temples; on the opposite end of the island from the lighthouse stood a conventional rectangular temple to Poseidon, God of the Sea, with no particularly promising hiding place; overlooking the landbridge there was another small temple, this time to Isis, equally unpromising. A short distance from the Isis temple was a small fort, but this was well-guarded. The lighthouse was also well-guarded; it was planted in the courtyard of a huge square fortress. On the fortress walls we could see soldiers in Roman uniforms pacing back and forth, and more soldiers stood at the entrance.

As I craned my neck to look up at the tower, another thought struck me. I said, "That lighthouse is going to make everything as bright as day."

"Not when the fog comes in," said Mary.

We spent the entire afternoon scouting the island, at last selecting a spot behind the corinthian columns of the Isis Temple, on the side away from the lighthouse. It was not very good, but it was the best hiding place we could find.

Having made our choice, we strolled once again toward the landbridge. "I want to pick out my boat while it's still day," Mary explained. She broke into a run, full of mischievous excitement in spite of everything.

I was content to walk.

I was dead tired and full of apprehension about the night's adventure. I would have insisted on calling the whole thing off, except that I had a kind of irrational faith that Mary's bold plans could never fail. They'd never failed yet!

So I was trudging along the dirt path from the Isis Temple, above and a considerable distance behind Mary's running figure, watching her long shadow do a burlesque of her movements. There were far fewer people on both the island and the landbridge than there had been an hour before, and those few were all drifting along in the same direction, heading for home. On the mainland, in the city, lights were being lit in anticipation of evening. Behind me the surf hissed and boomed; and a cold wind was rising, setting my cloak streaming and snapping, a wind that smelled of storm and electricity as well as salt and rotting fish. It seemed to be saying, "There will be no fog tonight."

At the far end of the island, at the Temple of Poseidon, a conch shell honked a mournful warning that night was coming. Some of the homeward-bound figures walked faster.

And then, from the direction of the lighthouse, I heard the beat of horse's hooves. I turned my head, saw a squad of mounted Roman soldiers riding toward me at a medium canter, the horses' tails and manes and the soldiers' cloaks twisting out to one side in the wind. I neither stopped nor broke into a run. Many soldiers had passed me today, but not one had bothered to look at me. I slogged on, head down, shoulders hunched, not wasting another glance on the soldiers, though it had become clear they were coming in my direction, that they would undoubtedly pass me on this trail.

When they had almost reached me, I moved to the side of the path to let them pass.

Then, quite clearly in the stillness of dusk, I heard a laugh, and the words, in English, "Oh, that's capital, Lestrade!"

Lestrade!

I turned my head at last.

The first man, the one who was speaking, was dressed in such ornately decorated armor I could not doubt he was some important official. Beside him rode a smaller, thinner man; in spite of the tunic, cloak, sandals and short-sword, I recognized Inspector Lestrade of Scotland Yard.

Then Beggars Could Ride

His narrow face was thrown back, his teeth were showing. He was laughing!

I saw him clearly, but, though he rode past me at a distance of less than three feet, he did not see me, or at least did not recognize me. With a sick horror I thought, *Of course Lestrade is here. We've done exactly what he might have expected us to do.* I was a sailor. This was a seaport, the only major port, besides Sherlock, in the area. Of course! *Elementary, my dear Lestrade!*

A moment later the squad of soldiers passed me, riding roughly two abreast, their weathered features frozen in an expression of bored brutality.

Beyond Lestrade and the official I could see Mary pausing before going out on the bridge, looking back. She must have heard the horses.

She was alone. There was no one else anywhere near her.

In spite of the native costume, in spite of the veil, there was something about her movements, something about her figure . . . she was, unmistakably, herself!

Lestrade gave a shout and pointed at her, reining up abruptly. The official reined up beside him, turned in his saddle, and shouted something in Latin to the squad of soldiers.

One of the soldiers detached himself from the squad and, urging his horse to a gallop, thundered past Lestrade and on down the path toward the bridge. Mary stood still, facing us.

At this point Mary had a choice.

She could not run to the left. The small fort blocked her escape in that direction. But she could run to the right, down the narrow sandy beach where the horse would find the muck and stones hard going. This would give her a small though real chance of escape, but it would have the disadvantage of leading the soldiers back in my direction.

Or she could not run at all, surrendering without a struggle. This would not lead the soldiers toward me, but would not lead them away either.

Or she could do what she did do.

She ran out onto the bridge, heedless of the fact that the horseman could not fail to overtake her there.

The official gave another command, and the whole squad broke into a gallop in the direction of the bridge.

I stood frozen, helpless, watching.

Oh how she ran! Her cowl fell back, letting her golden hair stream behind her in the sullen glowering red light from the setting sun. Oh, how she ran! Her veil came loose, fell off. I could not clearly see her face at this distance, yet I could have sworn there was a defiant tilt to her chin, a tilt that seemed to say that even now she had a scheme, knew a way, had a trick, was about to. . . .

Yes, she ran amazingly fast.

But the horse ran faster.

How easily, how effortlessly he closed in on her!

The rider leaned out of his saddle, way over to one side. He was going to snatch her up, hold her struggling body in front of him as he, laughing, brought her to his commanding officer. I could almost read his mind, that horseman.

Mary's sandal came loose.

She tripped, fell.

The horse went over her, almost but not quite avoiding stepping on her. As in a slow motion movie I saw a hoof strike her head.

A little way beyond her, the horseman reined up.

She lay on the landbridge, perfectly still, her head twisted at an angle impossible for a person who is alive.

The official gave a scream of rage. Lestrade spurred his horse to greater speed. And I, at last, turned and fled, stumbling up the trail toward the lighthouse.

I fell several times, because it was hard to see where I was going through all those tears.

CHAPTER 14

When I had wanted to live, it had been difficult to find a hiding place on the island. Now, when I no longer cared for life, it was easy.

Only half-aware of what I was doing, I staggered to the wall surrounding the lighthouse, then followed the wall to the edge of the cliff overlooking the rushing, thundering surf. I hesitated only a moment before slipping over the brink and sliding with a rush, down the wet, slippery rocks. Would something stop me before I hit the water? I didn't care. The Black Ecstasy gave me that total indifference that has so often, in so many lives, supplied a counterfeit of courage.

There was a ledge! It broke my fall and almost broke my back. I lay there among the rocks, panting. A wave exploded at my feet, drenching me. I scrambled for higher ground as another wave and yet another clutched at me and missed narrowly.

Slowly, carefully, I crept along the face of the cliff, working my way farther and farther out along the side of the island toward the sea. Above me loomed the high, massive wall surrounding the lighthouse, actually a seawall built of cyclopean blocks, meant to withstand, not the puny assaults of men, but the repeated battering-ram blows of the ocean. When there was a storm, the sea would crash directly against those walls and the stretch of natural rock along which I crawled would be under water most of the time.

I had thought I sensed a storm coming, yet I'd hidden in a place that a storm would turn into a death trap. Was my lemming-urge to suicide cured, as I'd thought, or simply waiting, waiting for some unbearable emotional pain to give it a new excuse? Yet things were different now from what they had been. I had not simply given myself up, indifferent to the death penalty that would surely await me. Nor had I rushed with false and futile heroism to Mary's rescue, forcing the soldiers to use their swords on me, rendering her act of self-sacrifice meaningless. (I am certain in my mind that she did what she did with her usual bold decisiveness. She had meant to draw the soldiers away from me, knowing she would be captured, not knowing she would die.)

I'd changed. The lemming-urge was there, but I was using it, making it help me to escape, to live. There might be a storm, yes, but then again there might not!

I could not see the lighthouse itself, but I knew it was there. As the sunlight faded, the bright steady glow from the tower top replaced it, illuminating the heaving sea and whitecaps a short distance away, but leaving me and the rest of the seawall face in shadow. If anyone were to look along the wall, there was a good chance their night-vision would be ruined by that light, so that I would be invisible. The light did not rotate, as on a modern lighthouse, but remained fixed, perhaps directed by mirrors out toward the sea.

I paused and rested, wedging myself in a crevice. Above the hiss and roar of the water I heard distant shouts. Looking back the way I had come, I saw torches. Evidently the soldiers were searching the island. I held myself perfectly still, so that their eyes would not be attracted by movement, and waited. Would one of them shout something triumphantly in Latin? Would the few torches I now saw be joined by others? Would heads appear along the edge of the seawall, above me?

No. The torches moved back and were lost to view around the corner of the wall. The soldiers had not seen me and had not believed I was insane enough to be where I was.

I was cold and wet, but the wind was without pity. I drew my cape close around me, but found it badly torn and so wet it was almost worse than nothing. There was, moreover, no way to get dry, as each new wave spattered me with more spray, and there was a fine mist that never abated. This mist was caused, I think, by narrow fissures from which, every time a wave was on the rise, miniature geysers would erupt with a sound like a human sigh, creating temporary ghosts made of tiny droplets of water. There was a real possibility I had escaped the soldiers only to die of exposure.

All the same, as Mary would have done, I forced myself to think, to examine my situation from every angle. I had to escape, if for no other reason than to justify her sacrifice. If it turned out such a girl had died for nothing, it would be an insult to the universe!

First, I had to assume Lestrade had set guards on the island end of the landbridge, that he'd called out all the

Then Beggars Could Ride

available troops to search the island for me. It would not be wise for me to retrace my steps and try to cross the island or the bridge on foot.

Second, knowing that I was a sailor, he would undoubtedly set a guard on the fishing boats, and would have biremes rowing back and forth in the harbor, ready to pursue and catch any suspicious boat heading for open sea. These biremes would also move along the shore, keeping an eye out for swimmers, but here on the seaward side of the island they'd never come in very close for fear of the rocks.

Could I swim back to the city of Isis?

The actual swimming would not be difficult, but thanks to that confounded lighthouse I would be bound to be seen by the patroling biremes as soon as I came up for air, and I could not swim the whole distance underwater. With a good fog I'd have a chance, but the fog Mary had hoped for would not appear as long as the weather remained as it was.

A third point: once in the city, would I be able to find the Christians again? I did not know the city at all well, and could not speak the Alexandrian languages, and in my wet, torn clothing I would stick out like a sore thumb, only to be spotted easily by the first soldier who passed me.

Could I expect help?

Mary had told the Christians not to expect us back; they would not be looking for me. The techs had no way of knowing where I was, and even if they found out somehow, would not provoke an open confrontation with the local authorities by attempting my rescue. What about Captain Marlinspike? From him least of all could I expect help. He'd told me as much. In a few hours he would put to sea, neither knowing nor caring what had become of me.

Yes, I knew his habits.

He'd set sail shortly before dawn, weather permitting, and when he was out of the pseudo-Thames and well into the Pacific, he'd swing southward, keeping about two miles from shore, as he always did except when there was a storm brewing. Yes, that's what he'd do. The wind was right for it, strong but not too strong, and from the right direction.

Suddenly I realized something.

I would see *The Flying Dutchman*. I would see it

clearly as it passed me, two miles out, in the light of the rising sun.

Then I knew what I must do.

MARY was dead and yet not dead.

I had become her.

No, I was not a woman, and I had not learned to steal without hesitation as she had, but her clear mind, as it winked out in her poor crushed skull, seemed to have miraculously been reincarnated in my own muddled head. I had wept for her at first, but I wept no longer. One weeps for what is lost, not for what one has newly gained and will retain until the end. Also, thinking with my new clear brain, I understood that though she loved me, though she had given her life for me, Mary would not have wept if I had been the one to die.

Instead of weeping, I schemed.

A clipper ship does not actually go very fast, when one thinks of the speeds of trains or aircraft, but it goes faster than a man can swim. I did some careful mental arithmetic. I did it again, changing the factors slightly. There could be no mistake. To rendezvous with the ship two miles out, I would have to begin swimming before the ship was in sight.

This introduced another hazard. If, for some reason, the ship did not set sail, I would find myself two miles out to sea, completely alone. Or what if the captain, on a whim, decided to sail one mile out, or three? Or what if I miscalculated the distance? Or what if the ocean currents upset my calculations? There were risks, but I did not give up, as I might have before. Mary wouldn't have given up.

I waited, wedged in the crevice, watching the sky for traces of the first light of dawn. That would be my signal.

The sky was clear. The stars shone. The moon, if there was a moon, was not within the sector of sky I could see from my hiding place. The wind remained fairly constant. There was no fog. There was no storm. The surf remained constant. It must have been an illusion, but I felt warmer. I worked myself into a more comfortable position and seemed to see Mary in a garden, waving to me, wearing her starched Victorian dress.

I jerked awake, an instant before tumbling down to the surf-pounded rocks below me. I had, it seemed, yet another enemy.

Then Beggars Could Ride

Sleep, simple sleep. Sleep could kill me, as surely as any of my other foes, human or inanimate. Yet I was so tired, so bone-weary.

But I did not sleep. Mary would not have slept.

I moved about from rock to rock, keeping awake by keeping moving, though movement on these slippery surfaces was yet another hazard.

As the hours oozed by, I gradually worked my way to the tip of the island, where the seawall bent at right angles toward the mainland. From here I could see a portion of the city of Isis and part of the sheltered harbor. As I had expected, torch-lit boats were moving to and fro, looking for me, and the reflections of the torches danced in the choppy water. None of them ventured close to me, or headed out into the heavy sea beyond the point where I was crouching.

Once I heard voices and cowered back into the shadows as a pair of heads appeared on the top of the seawall above me, backlit by the lighthouse. I was not seen, and soon the heads went away.

On the mainland too there were moving lights; torches, lanterns. I was causing a lot of excitement.

The chief thing was that from here I could see the eastern sky where the first trace of dawn would appear.

When it did appear, at long last, it came on so slowly that at first I was not aware of it. The clue that tipped me off was the colors of the rocks around me. They were no longer gray, but streaked with an infinite variety of subdued color. I looked up. The sky, though all the stars were still showing, was no longer black, but an indescribable purple, dark yet luminous. If I waited longer, I would certainly be seen from the boats or from the lighthouse tower.

I stripped and, choosing the most outcropping boulder I could find as my springboard, dove naked into the sea.

The first few seconds were the most dangerous. I was almost smashed against the rocks by first one wave, then another. But then I was past the worst part, swimming harder than I'd ever done before, and soon I was beyond the breakers, floating on my back, looking up at the lighthouse. There were men walking along the walls of the fort that surrounded the lighthouse, men standing on the high parapet next to the light, men on the lower parapet that separated the broad lower tower from the narrow upper tower. None of them broke into a run, pointed fingers, waved arms. I had not been seen.

The tower, then, was my friend.

In fact, without that tower to use as a reference point, I don't know how I could have maintained my course toward that imaginary X two miles out where, if no one of an infinite number of things went wrong, I would rendezvous with the *Dutchman*.

I rolled over and went into a breaststroke, pacing myself, taking my time, conserving my strength.

Two miles is a long way to swim, when you haven't slept.

THE sunrise was magnificent, worthy of being announced by a heavenly choir singing the Hallelujah Chorus. Under the circumstances all that could be managed was a single seagull, squawking harshly as he circled overhead, speculating, perhaps, on how long it would be before I became edible.

I floated on my back, watching him pass and repass as I gently rose and fell with the motion of the swells. Saltwater filled my mouth. I blew it out, thinking of a whale spouting. I was worried.

One thing I had not realized was how little one can see when one's eyes are almost level with the ocean. From the crest of a wave I could usually, but not always, locate the tower. In the wave troughs I could see the wave on one side of me and the wave on the other and between them, the sky. That was all, except for the gull, and now even the gull, after one last pass, abandoned me. I had hoped to maintain a course by lining up the tower with something on the mainland, but had soon given this up when I realized that all I could see was the tower itself and some featureless distant mountains.

I was moving away from the tower, that was certain, but at an angle to my hoped-for course. How great an angle I had no way of knowing, though it seemed from the changing position of the mountains I must be drifting south.

The thing that bothered me most was the realization that the *Flying Dutchman* would have to pass quite close or I would not see it. Its rigging was tall, but not tall enough to be seen even from the crests of the waves if it

Then Beggars Could Ride

were more than a mile away. Would I at least hear it? A great hush was over the sea, broken only by the cries of the gulls and a faint splashing at the wave crests. I should be able to hear something.

But then my ears were so often under water, particularly when I was drifting on my back, and when I was swimming I made a splashing that probably wasn't very loud objectively, but sounded loud enough to me to mask any other sound.

It would be only too easy for the ship to glide past me, unseen and unheard. Had it already done so?

No! I wouldn't accept that!

I sucked in air, rolled over and began swimming again.

THE old me, the drunk, the weakling, could never have gotten this far. The old me would have drowned an hour ago, shortly after sunrise.

Now the new me also was revealing his limitations. The periods of swimming had become steadily shorter, the periods of drifting longer. I was weary. I was winded. In my mind the mog was whispering messages of fatalism to an increasingly receptive audience. For example: "Channel swimmers are always accompanied by a boat. Where's your boat, little man?"

Worst of all, I had lost track of the tower.

A minute ago it had dawned on me that I hadn't seen it for some time. I had wasted a good deal of energy in frantic search, bursts of thrashing that raised my head a few extra precious inches above the ocean, timed to synchronize with those instants when I was on a wave crest.

The result: I was no longer certain of the direction of land. The position of the sun gave me some guidance, but in those moments of thrashing at the crests, I had been unable to be sure of the difference between my distant mountains and certain low cloud formations on the horizon.

I drifted, pondering my situation, gazing at the bright empty morning sky.

Question: Suppose I miss the ship. Will I be able to swim back to land?

I moved my body slightly.

It protested.

The answer was no.

Second question: If I stop swimming and confine myself to floating, how long will I last?

Answer: With luck, another hour.

Question: Why are wave troughs so long and wave crests so short?

Answer: To torture fools who swim out too far.

Then I seemed to see Mary again, fading into my consciousness. She was saying, "Don't be such a poop!"

I closed my eyes, trying to see her more clearly.

When I opened them again I was at a wave crest and there, bearing swiftly down on me, was *The Flying Dutchman*.

It was so close that even from the trough I could see its crow's nest and part of the topgallant mast. How had it gotten so close without my seeing it? Had I actually passed out for a moment there?

No matter! Here it was!

I began wildly waving my arms and screaming, "Help! Help! Help!"

Now I could hear the thump and swish of the waves as the bow cut through them, the creak of the masts, see some of the sailors perched on the yardarms.

"Help!" I shouted. "Help!"

Nobody was looking in my direction.

I splashed with all my strength, my cries becoming frantic, wordless.

Now the ship was passing me, so close the shadow of the sails crossed me for an instant.

"Help!" I had again developed the power of speech.

But the ship had passed.

The spreading wake hit me, breaking over my head, filling my nostrils, my lungs. A terrible undertow dragged me down into the green shimmering water, into the whirling clouds of bubbles, into the darkness below.

CHAPTER 15

I knew I was weak, that was all.

My eyes fluttered open.

I was looking at the dimly illuminated underside of an upper bunk. I frowned. How puzzling!

With considerable effort I raised myself to a sitting position and looked around. I recognized the bunkroom of the *Dutchman*. The other bunks were empty. I was, it seemed, alone. Sunlight filtering in through the portholes told me it was day. The faint, almost imperceptible movement of the ship told me we were in port, probably moored to some dock. The heat told me it was probably a tropic port.

I gathered my strength and called out, "Hello! Is anyone here?"

There were swift footsteps in the passageway and Captain Marlinspike Werner poked his head in the door, looking at me with surprise through his steel-rim spectacles. He wore his usual visored cap but, thanks to the heat, had exchanged his peacoat for a white, slightly soiled T-shirt. "Well," said he, "I see you've decided to talk like a human being."

"What do you mean?"

He pulled up a chair at my bunkside and sat down. "Don't you remember a thing? You've been delirious with fever for almost a week."

"All that time? You—!"

"That's right. I've seen hangovers, but. . . ." He rolled his eyes. Suddenly he leaned forward and asked, "Who's Mary?"

"A girl."

"Aye, and she must be quite a girl at that, from the way you were talking. I'm surprised you came back to the ship at all, let alone come back the way you did, almost killing yourself."

"She's dead."

"Oh, well, I'm sorry." He was embarrassed.

"Never mind. Just tell me, where are we?"

"We're at anchor in the harbor of Acapulco, in Mexico."

"And where's the crew?"

"On shore leave. Acapulco isn't like Los Angeles. It's

got open enclaves, no papers needed. You should have waited—"

I closed my eyes. "I'm glad I didn't. But how did I get on the ship?"

"Don't you remember that, either?"

"I remember I was drowning."

"Well, at that time I was sitting on the afterdeck, sunning meself, when I thought I heard someone yell. I looked back and there, sticking out of the wake, were two arms. I wasted no time, sir, but kicked off my shoes and shouted 'Man overboard', then jumped into the sea. I can assure you, the ship hove to and came about smartly with the captain in the drink!" He chuckled. "I dove down and slapped a grip on you, and when the longboat came for us, I dragged you out of the sea like a drowned rat and pumped the water out of you with these two thumbs." He showed me his thumbs. "They're magic thumbs, Mr. McClintok. Yours is not the only life they've saved."

"Thank you, Captain," I murmured.

"It's the least I could do for a man who wants that bad to join my ship." He touched my arm. "The crew'll be telling this story for years, long after the both of us has died of old age. Now, of course, you're more than ever welcome to sail with us!"

I considered that for a long time, so long that he gave my arm a little shake and said, "You awake?"

"I'm awake, but I won't be sailing with you."

"What?" He was dumbfounded. "After all that—"

"After all that." I nodded slowly.

"Are you going back to Sherlock?"

"No."

"One of the other Los Angeles enclaves?"

"No."

"Are you goin' home to your wife?"

"No."

"But, what else is there?"

"One thing."

He was at his wit's end. "And what may that be?"

"I'm going to become a tech."

He frowned and shook his head. "Oh no, oh no, you don't want that. Nothin' but trouble, trouble all the time." I looked at him, trying to think how to explain, but I didn't have the energy to go into a long involved argument about something that was, to me, so simple. Of

Then Beggars Could Ride

course there would be trouble. Of course there would be work. Of course there would be painful decisions, tension, moral puzzles that could not be solved but must be. Of course there would be errors of judgment, bitter regrets, innocent people hurt, sometimes killed. Of course. Of course. Someday, as the Christians believed, God might come to Earth and take command, putting an end to trouble and mistakes, creating a true utopia.

In the meantime, someone had to mind the store.

After the Captain had gone, I lay awake a long time, though I was very tired, thinking about a world that was not heaven, but only a mim of heaven, and thinking about Mary.

Being a tech was not her dream. She'd wanted only to go to sea. But after going to sea, what then?

She too would have sooner or later seen that she must become a tech, that it was the next logical step for her, and she would have let nothing on Earth stand in her way.

I was sure of it.

And the Mary within me considered this carefully before saying, *"Mahleestah!"*

PART THREE

CHAPTER 16

The Metropolitan Cathedral had been torn down; in its place stood an Aztec temple. The National Palace (*Palacio Nacional*) also was gone; on its site had been built a replica of the ancient Palace of Montezuma. These buildings stood in the midst of a city called Tenochtitlan, "Place of the High Priest Tenoch," on an island in the center of a lake called Mexliapan, "Lake of the Moon."

This lake, in its turn, was the center of Mexico City, a vast megapolis that seemed, from the cliff where I sat, like a floor of hexagonal tiles bounded on all sides by mountains. Each of the hexagons was a mim of a different time and place, but as I looked down on them through the shimmering haze of a hot afternoon, it was not their difference that impressed me, but their sameness. Surface details—what is called Style—change, but the nature of a city does not, because a city is built to satisfy human needs. Human needs are always and everywhere the same. Change was the mirage of twentieth-century men, a mirage that led them to, inadvertently, create a change none of them had desired, a change from a planet of plenty to a planet of permanent scarcity. In the twenty-first century man carefully cut up all history into small, digestible pieces; the rest of time would be occupied with slowly digesting these pieces.

Morality had not ended war. Morality had not ended waste. Morality had not ended nationality, pollution or overpopulation. It was scarcity that had ended them. It was scarcity that had ended change, challenging Man to create an environment that provided, not change, but a mim of change . . . simple variety. Robbed of change, man had reluctantly settled for utopia.

There was, I mused, an unbridgeable gulf between the people of my century and those of the previous century. Our great-grandparents, had had everything and had thrown it away. We had the used-up planet they left us, and we'd worked miracles with it. I thought of the old story of the broken sword. And I thought of the ancient Aztec. He was like me. He'd had the wheel (his toys prove it) and he hadn't used it.

I smiled and stood up, stretching.

I walked slowly back toward a cluster of whitewashed

Then Beggars Could Ride

huts irregularly perched on the mountainside, the village that had been my home for five years.

Walking felt good. I was used to steep trails full of rocks and potholes. I was used to this young man's body that diet, exercise, calmness and no vices had given me. As a young man I had had an old man's body, the result of a different lifestyle—a fundamental wrongness of which my drinking had been no more than a symptom. The wrongness had been symbolized by a mental fog, what I'd called Mog. (I'd learned that word, and the reality behind it, from Doc, my first psychotherapist.) The fog was almost gone now. I could see it clearly in my mind's eye, hold it back easily. I'd been told the time would come when the mog would leave me completely, never to return, and I could believe that. It was so much fainter than it had once been.

Would Doc have recognized me now?

Probably not.

He had seen the beginning of the change in me, but he had not seen what plastic surgery had done to my face, he had not heard how deep my voice had become, observed my neatly-trimmed black beard and hair, sensed the poise that daily meditation gave me.

Would Marge have recognized me?

Hardly likely! She knew me as Newton the Drunk. For five years I had not tasted alcohol or, for that matter, tobacco, coffee, tea, or even sugar. These things were not forbidden, but they had no hold on me, had no part in the self-transformation I was working on. I could have smoked marijuana if I'd liked, eaten peyote, LSD, swallowed all sorts of uppers or downers, but I did not. The path to inner freedom leads in the opposite direction.

Though the trail was still uphill, I broke into a run. If I had a vice, it was the joy that pounded in my flesh when my body performed its daily miracles of strength and endurance. I reached the village and, in spite of the thin air at this high altitude, wasn't even breathing hard.

(Did the ancient Aztec runners puff and wheeze as they carried the messages of Montezuma through these mountains?)

Laughing, I passed through a doorless doorway into the interior of one of the huts.

Doc Jumo, seated behind a battered table that served him as a desk, glanced up at me and said, "Hello, Jack."

I was still Jack to the techs. I had not yet gone through the ritual of formally choosing a new name.

"Ah, Jumo! I heard you wanted to speak to me." I threw myself down on a worn, sagging brown sofa.

He nodded seriously. "That's right."

Doc Jumo was a short, hefty, broad-shouldered Negro. (Was he born Black? I neither knew nor cared.) He seemed older than I was, though it was difficult to judge how much older.

I waited expectantly.

He began, "You want to become a tech?"

"You know I do."

"You could."

"When?"

"Now," he said, then amended, "Or as soon as you choose your new name."

I was not surprised. I had done well on recent tests. Others who had come here to begin training at the same time I had were becoming techs. I said, "Let me think a minute."

I had considered many names during my five years here, but had not made the final decision. "Think as long as you like," said Jumo. "Take a week, a month."

"A minute should be enough."

I'd been told I'd have a list of names to pick from. The only names available, now that the moment had come, were those already in my mind.

As if making casual conversation, Jumo said, "Have you found utopia yet?"

"I don't think utopia is a place anymore."

"What is it then?"

"It's an attitude."

"Bravo!" He clapped his hands as if I'd been doing a theatrical performance. Perhaps that's what it was: a theatrical performance. Indeed, the odd sort of training I got from the techs had shown me new meaning in the Shakespearean expression, "All the world's a stage." This village was a stage, certainly. It looked like a Mexican village; nobody passing through could have thought otherwise. Jumo and I and everyone else here dressed exactly like Mexican peasants, from bare feet to straw sombrero. It was a Mexican village, but it was also a school, or, looked at another way, a mental hospital.

He went on, "You have come to see utopia as we in the

Then Beggars Could Ride

Tech Corps do; not as civilians do. For most people utopia is something simple, a certain social system, a certain historical period, the realization of a certain ideal. Such people want things a certain way, want them to stay that way, and want them handed over on a platter, without any effort on their part. They don't want to be responsible, to make decisions that guide and shape their own lives. For them everything is the fault of the stars, of society, of history, of fate . . . anything but themselves. Give such a person the right mim, and he's content. It's this kind of people who are the overwhelming majority of the human race."

He leaned back with a sigh, looked over at me from under his straw hat, then continued, "For another group, a minority, this is not enough. You were in this minority group. You weren't content with a pre-programmed life. The mim that made everyone around you happy drove you to attempt suicide, and then to embark on a quest for a different lifestyle. For a while it was the quest itself that was your utopia.

"Finally," he said, "there is a third group, the smallest of all. To be in the third group, one must accept responsibility not only for one's own decisions, life-planning and welfare, but for the decisions, life-planning and welfare of others as well, the people around one, ultimately the whole of human society, including the society of the future. That is the role we techs play. Utopia for us is simply to do what needs doing.

"Twenty-first-century society, unlike every previous attempt at a good way of life, has succeeded. It has succeeded because, unlike its predecessors, it has taken these three types into account, made a place for them. In fact, it has made a place for all the infinite diversity of human nature. We've learned that our ancestors were making a mistake when they believed the height of a civilization is measured by the rate of energy consumption. It's actually measured by how well the civilization meets human needs, psychological as well as physical."

I interrupted, "I think I'll use Paul as my first name."

He smiled. "Any special reason?"

Half-jokingly I answered, "Because I feel I'll become an apostle of the tech viewpoint."

He chuckled, then asked, "What about your middle name?"

"Can I use a girl's name?"

"Certainly."

"My second name will be Mary. I knew someone by that name once, someone who taught me a lot about self-determination."

"Okay, now let's hear your last name."

"Rivers. That sounds gentle and flowing, a good name for a Doc."

"You're not a Doc yet." He was teasing me. "First a tech, then a Doc. You'll have years of training to finish before you take on your first Jack or Jill."

"Years of training? How many years?"

"You've asked that before. You know we never answer that kind of question."

"I was thinking I might be too old, by the time I graduate, to do any good."

He waved my fears away with a nonchalant hand. "If you live right, you'll live long. Most techs live to be well over a hundred, and remain active almost to the end. Now let's hear that name."

"Paul Mary Rivers," I said.

He got up. "Fine. Let's go to the director and make arrangements for your naming ceremony."

The ceremony, which took place the following Sunday night, was simple but impressive, involving everyone living at the village, techs, Docs, Jacks and Jills alike. (The majority of the village population was made up of patients.)

There was a procession, prayers, candles, and singing, all out under the stars near a big bonfire. This was the first part, involving, as I say, the whole village.

The second part of the ceremony began at midnight, and involved only the techs, no laymen. I would like to tell you about it: it was one of the most moving experiences of my life.

But I am sworn to secrecy.

CHAPTER 17

I was a tech, but I had no specialty. I must now learn to be a Doc, or mental therapist. I could have chosen to be a scientific farmer, or an engineer, or a mechanic, or a mim researcher, or even—God forbid—an assassin. I could have chosen to be satisfied with being a "cured" Jack and gone to live in one of many enclaves open to me. None of these lines of action held the challenge, for me, of psychotherapy.

Doc Jumo was my teacher.

The setting could be anywhere in the village, or in the surrounding mountains. The lessons came as the therapy had come to me before, so informally I hardly knew it was happening.

But I was learning at last the tech method, learning how to do everything while seeming to do nothing, and as I learned I understood, little by little, the firm but gentle process by which I had been brought to this point. I learned, for example, that I'd been spotted as a potential Doc in the very first psychological interview after my suicide attempt.

I learned the subliminal tricks that my first Doc had used on me, the elementary tools of the psych tech.

Jumo explained as he milked a goat.

"You've seen photos of the psychotherapists of the previous century. You've read their biographies. They were all sick men, physically and mentally, and for this reason were never effective, no matter what technique they used, no matter what theory they believed. The patient, no matter how insane, could always sense the doctor's weakness and thus could not respect the doctor or believe in the truth of the doctor's words. Our approach is different. Before I confront a patient, I make sure that I am myself in excellent health, physically and mentally. If I am fat, no fat man will believe I can help him. If I am unsure of myself, no neurotic will trust me. If I am taking drugs, no drug addict will think I know a way to, as they used to say, 'kick the monkey.' So today the psychotherapist is, before he is anything else, an athlete. The therapist is in training, as certainly as any football or baseball player."

"That's why all the Docs here do hard manual labor," I said.

He picked up the bucket of goat's milk. "Exactly. But the Doc must be yet more. Orthodox practitioners used to bemoan the public's fondness for quacks. Actually, the quacks were doing something right. They must have been, since their record for cures was better than that of the orthodox therapists. The thing they were doing right was projecting mental images, not so much in an obvious way, but in the theatrical presentation they made to each patient in their manner, their voice. Today we have learned more from the quacks than from the orthodox, who were actually only quacks of another sort. Today we, too, put on a good show. So the second thing the therapist is before he is a therapist is an actor."

"Are there more?"

"Many more. Among those called quacks by the orthodox were various sorts of holy man. These gurus, swamis, masters, and warlocks were doing something right, too. They were mastering themselves before attempting to master others. Today the therapist practises some sort of meditation technique, so that he never faces a Jack or Jill without a calm and balanced soul. Before he is a therapist, then, he is an Enlightened One."

"But we haven't said anything yet about the patient."

"The patient is not important. By stepping into the role of patient, he surrenders himself to someone else's will, ceases to be a full human being. Therefore his role in the therapy becomes passive. He expects to become a slave. And so he does become a slave. We don't want to know his petty problems. We don't want to know his boring biography. We don't want to know his dirty little secrets. It is the therapist who is important, who is, in fact, all-important. The patient will do a mim, so far as he is able, of the therapist, so all the therapist must do to cure the patient is become someone worth copying. Even if the therapist does nothing at all, the patient will, from subliminal cues of voice and mannerism, understand and imitate. That is why I never seem to do any work, yet my patients keep getting better. I have done all my work before I see the patient. By that time I either am worth imitating or not."

"Is that what's called non-directive therapy?"

"Not at all! Non-directive therapy is a hoax. More often than not, patient and doctor trade places. The doctor gets worse instead of the patient getting better, because the patient usually has more imagination and the doctor gets caught up, begins to do a mim of madness!"

And, there beside the barn, he gleefully showed me how a patient, given half a chance, can turn the tables on the doctor. It was a disturbing demonstration for someone who had been, as I had, so recently a patient. I played the doctor and he the clever madman. In minutes he had me contradicting myself, babbling nonsense, losing self-control.

But when he saw my confusion he stopped and, laughing, added, "It's better that I do this to you than some patient. Patients don't know when to quit."

I LEARNED quickly.

It was not years, but months, before I began to do therapy, first in a small way, as a back-up for Jumo, then, more and more, on my own. The tech teaching method had few sharp dividing lines. One did not graduate from Class A, then enter Class B. Instead Jumo fed me responsibility one spoonful at a time, as he thought I was ready, and I continually surprised myself with my progress. I soon realized that there was almost nothing of a verbal or written nature to learn. The whole training program was like a course in judo: there were certain simple movements, certain actions, which had to be practised and practised until they became reflexes. There was a time to nod and a time to laugh and a time to speak sharply; a time to confide in the patient, a time to act like a rat, a time to close down and quit, or to table for later. It took energy, concentration, endurance—yes—but hardly any brains at all.

Tech psychotherapy had its textbooks, but nobody in the village read them. Dealing with the human mind was not like consulting an encyclopedia and coming up with answers, but like playing tennis. Not chess! Tennis! What was in the books?

I dipped into them from time to time, and found them filled with idiotic platitudes and murky generalizations, all in a style that clearly showed the author knew he was talking nonsense.

The therapy given patients in the village was a matter

of providing an environment that favored self-healing, an environment that was deliberately primitive and hard, but simple and predictable, an environment cut off from the outside world; then placing, among the large number of Jacks and Jills, a few techs to serve as "friends" and role models. It wasn't much, unless you compared it with the snake pits and drug dens of previous eras. The techs would no more think of using lobotomy, shock-treatment or continuous chemo-therapy than they would of using an iron maiden, or a rack.

Of course, on the other side of the coin, a patient who was judged a hopeless case could be taken out and shot, though this never happened while I was there.

The tech psychotherapy approaches with confidence the kind of cases previous therapies could do little with. My first case was a drug addict. Because I had been an alcoholic and had licked it, the junkie was fairly easy. Or perhaps one gets better at the Doc game by playing it a while. The junkie (a lady junkie, by the way) married one of the techs after her ceremony of naming, and they moved away.

Then came others, all resolved successfully. I sensed that my abilities would only continue to grow as time passed.

I was rapidly becoming a respected member of the therapeutic community. Other techs, when they couldn't hack it, sent for me. I was, in an informal way, the second highest "court of appeals" in the village, Jumo being the first.

And now we come to my next case.

I must pause now. This one will not be easy to talk about.

AROUND noon, when I checked in to his hut, Doc Jumo told me a new Jill was coming.

"What's her name?" I asked without interest.

"A Mrs. Patroni. You want to take her case?"

"Okay."

The name sounded vaguely familiar, but I dismissed it from my mind and went out into the sunlight to make my rounds. I was working with the other techs on five cases, two Jacks and three Jills. My case load was increasing steadily, but Jumo made sure I didn't take on more than I could handle.

Then Beggars Could Ride

At about one o'clock I sat near the cliff that overlooks Mexico City with one of my Jills, talking quietly about how, according to her, she was possessed by a demon who forced her to eat rhododendrons.

"I kind of like the taste of them myself," she was admitting in a dreamy voice. She was an attractive girl, as schizophrenics go, with wide wondering blue eyes that saw things other eyes could not. She added, "Even without the demon, I might have a blossom now and then, for dessert."

I yawned. "No harm in that."

Yes, she was an attractive girl, thin as a high-fashion model. Rhododendrons, I decided, weren't fattening.

"I hear you're going to be working on the new Jill," she said wistfully.

"That's right."

"I hope she won't be a more interesting case than I am. She might distract you, and without you to hold him back, there's no telling what my demon might do. He may not always be satisfied with rhododendrons, you know." She was looking at my throat.

I thought, *Typical schizo veiled threat*. I closed my eyes.

"Here she comes!" cried the Jill, jumping to her feet and pointing as my eyes popped open.

I sat up and looked in the direction she indicated. Below and slightly less than a mile away seven donkeys were slowly plodding up the steep trail, single file. Four techs were walking along with them, and on the back of the largest donkey sat a woman dressed in a long gray skirt and gray blouse. Her hair, which hung in ragged tangles to her shoulders, was gray too.

There was something familiar about her.

I shaded my eyes and squinted.

No use. She was too far away.

I glanced at the Jill beside me. She was pouting. "She's not here yet, and already you are hers."

I didn't answer.

She said, "My demon tells me to go talk to Doc Jumo."

I said nothing, but went on squinting.

"I hope you don't mind," said the Jill.

I said hurriedly, "No, no, that's all right."

I heard her footsteps running off toward the village.

The donkey train trudged out of sight behind a tall shaft of rock. I waited. Half an hour later the donkeys reappeared, one by one, much closer. The woman in gray sat like a gaunt corpse in her saddle, her body rigid, her eyes seeming to stare at nothing.

A catatonic trance, I thought. This would be a tough case. It would not be easy even to communicate with a woman who had switched off the world. But why did she look so familiar?

Where had I seen her before?

Abruptly I recognized her.

It was Marge.

CHAPTER 18

Jumo was unconvinced. Leaning back in the rickety cane-bottomed chair behind a battered table, he surveyed me quizzically from beneath his broad-brimmed straw hat. His black forehead glistened with sweat, but he wasted no precious energy wiping it dry. My own straw hat was in my hands, clutched to my chest, in the proper attitude of supplication, as I stood before him in the sweltering heat of midmorning. There were flies in the hut; I was uncomfortably aware of their sonorous hum as I waited for him to speak, aware also of the roughness of the wood planks under my bare feet, of the texture of the white shirt plastered with sweat to my back, of the smell of dust, decay and refried beans, of the salty taste of my own sweat as it trickled over my lips.

At last he sighed and said, "There's something you don't understand."

I answered, too quickly, "It's you who don't understand! I can't treat this woman. She used to be my wife."

He looked up at me, sadness in his glittering black eyes. "She used to be the wife of Newton McClintok. You are Paul Mary Rivers, a completely different person."

"Not *completely* different."

"Then we made a mistake when we allowed you to go through the ceremony of The New Name. Your membership in the techs is void, because it was obtained by fraud. That's too bad. I thought you had the makings of a Doc. You've been doing so well—"

"There's no fraud! Believe me, I—"

He nodded slowly. "No deliberate fraud perhaps."

"I *am* Paul Rivers."

He smiled. "Then there's no problem. Paul Rivers is an apprentice Psych Doc, a promising one at that. He should welcome a chance to practise on an interesting Jill. I shouldn't tell him this, but success with this Jill will undoubtedly lead to promotion. Try this name on for size. *Doc* Paul Rivers."

I was stunned into silence for a moment, then I said, "But what if I fail?"

He shrugged. "I will fail along with you, because, as your superior, I believed you were ready for this. We'd both be due for some extra training, both have to earn our titles all over again. It could take years. But you won't fail. I know you won't. You've had five years here as a Jack, and you got a lot of unintentional training then in addition to what you've gotten since graduation. It seeps in, you know. It's there. When you need it, you'll be able to count on it."

"And what if I refuse?"

"A tech enjoys a great deal of freedom, my friend, as you must have noticed, but nobody enjoys absolute freedom. This is the thing you don't understand. You don't have the right to say no to me." His voice had grown cold, distant, as it always did when he gave me a glimpse of the claws within the soft tech paw.

"If you put it that way," I said, grudgingly.

He leaned forward, rested his elbows on his table. "Have you looked at yourself in the mirror recently? I swear to you that in your physical appearance there's no trace of that person called Newton McClintok. He was weak. You are strong. He was old. You are young. He was a coward. You are, unless I am making a great mistake, a man of courage, a man who delights in a challenge, who seeks out problems and obstacles to test his mind and body, to teach him things, to give him exercise. You are no Newton. There is no Newton. Not any more."

I searched myself, my inner self. He was almost right. There was, at the very edge of my consciousness, still a trace of something that belonged to the Late Newton McClintok.

There was mog.

It was faint, it was feeble, but it was there.

I said, "You're sure I can handle this case?"

He said, "I'm staking my career on it."

I looked into his dark serious face. A lifetime of training and experience seemed written in those firm, hard features. Jumo was not a man who made decisions lightly.

"I'll do my best," I whispered.

He sprang up, shook my hand vigorously. "That's the spirit! I knew you wouldn't let me down."

As I stepped through Jumo's doorway into the glaring sunlight, my mind was already racing ahead, making plans.

I felt great! And the mog?

The mog had retreated a wee bit more.

Then Beggars Could Ride

Doc Karina, in peasant skirt and blouse, with dark hair and horn-rim glasses, was in her early twenties. She played with the ends of her hair as she talked. "Mrs. Patroni is on intravenous feeding. I haven't been able to get her to accept spoon-feeding," she said.

"I see," I said. Karina and I were standing in the glaring sunlight outside Marge's hut. It was the afternoon of the same day Jumo had given me the case.

Karina went on, "She hasn't spoken one word since she came to the village."

I thought, *There was a time when I'd have called that a blessing.* I said, "Too bad, but of course we know that sometimes a catatonic hears everything we say but doesn't feel moved to answer."

Karina nodded. "I've been talking to her, though it's all one way, and some of the Jills have babbled nonsense to her. The idea is to give her input, whether she reacts or not. Are you going to have a try?"

I held up Marge's dossier, a slender legal-size file folder I'd gotten from Central Records. "Jumo put me in charge of her."

"In charge, eh? Lots of luck!" Her tone was ironic.

I left Karina and went into Marge's hut.

It was a little cooler and a lot dimmer there. Marge sat cross-legged on the bed like a skinny Buddha, wearing the same gray clothing I'd seen when she arrived in the village. A long translucent plastic tube connected a vein in her arm with a glass bottle hanging inverted from a hook on the ceiling. Her blue, slightly bloodshot, eyes were open, but they did not focus on me as I crossed her field of vision. There was nothing about her to suggest the party girl, the flapper I'd known. Her gray hair was particularly disturbing; perhaps she'd had gray hair before, but her peroxide had hidden it.

I said, "Hello, Mrs. Patroni. I'm Paul Rivers."

She said nothing. After a while she blinked. She was otherwise motionless, but the blink proved she was alive, together with the faint, hardly noticeable rise and fall of her narrow chest.

I asked, "May I chat awhile?"

No reply.

I sat down on a dull red three-legged stool by her bedside and opened her dossier. I scanned it. It was horrifying, one of those life stories so ghastly they become funny. It would have been acceptable tech procedure to close the book and simply sit there. I chose to continue the interview. "Your name is Mrs. Leonard Patroni, isn't it?"

Silence.

"I see Leonard Patroni is your second husband. Your first husband was a fellow named Newton McClintok." I studied her face for some twitch of recognition. There was none. "And you had a daughter. Her name was Ruth. Is that right?"

No answer.

"Let's see now, was Newton Ruth's real father?" I thought, *Answer me that!*

Marge's expression remained totally blank.

"Was he?" I insisted.

She did not say.

I frowned. "Hmm. It seems Newton abandoned you. Have you any idea why? No?" I was skimming the case history, not reading it in detail. "You remarried. Mr. Patroni, your second husband, also abandoned you. Your daughter eloped. Your parents, who had been living with you, transferred to a different enclave. You bought a dog. He bit you." I thought, *I never realized it before Marge, but you're a real loser.*

I read on. "You began drinking more and more heavily, went through a series of boyfriends, lost a series of jobs, went on welfare." I stared at her for a while. It was hard to believe this kewpie doll had done all the the wild things in her case history, had actually suffered.

I read more. "You smoked marijuana daily, developed respiratory difficulties, which you blamed first on bronchitis, then, when they got worse, on a capitalist plot. You smoked more marijuana, developed more respiratory difficulties, became convinced you were a victim of germ warfare, that the Rockefeller family was spraying bacteria on your corn flakes. You bought a pistol for defense, smoked more marijuana, practised shooting cans off your backyard fence, missed the cans, and shot off your left big toe." I glanced over at her. Her left foot was tucked away under her, but I had no doubt the toe would be missing. To this recital of her misfortunes she had not reacted in any way. I probably could have dragged her mutilated foot out and had a look at it without her putting up the slightest resistance, but I didn't.

Then Beggars Could Ride

I went back to my reading. "At the hospital you attacked an orderly, accusing him of being one of Rockefeller's hired killers, thus bringing yourself to the attention of the psych tech in residence. You told the tech your story and he advised you to stop smoking marijuana, so you knocked him out with a bust of Sigmund Freud and made a break for it. When caught at the hospital exit, you went into catatonia. The locals were unable to bring you out of it, so you ended up here."

I closed the dossier and set it on the floor.

I said gravely, "Well, Marge, do you have anything to say for yourself?"

She didn't.

Hours later, when Karina came back, I was hoarse from talking, but Marge had yet to utter a single syllable.

IT was some morning or other. I'd lost all track of time. Jumo called me to his hut.

He said, "Has she spoken?"

I said, "Well, er, no."

"It's been two weeks."

"That long?"

"That long."

"I'm working on it, Jumo."

"Maybe someone else should work on it instead."

"What? I thought you told me you were staking your career on me."

"Could be I can save my career by staking it on someone else."

"Like who, for instance?"

"Karina."

"She's too young."

"I could work on it myself."

"Jumo, please, give me more time."

"How much time?"

"A month?"

"Too long."

"A week?"

"I'll give you until tomorrow morning."

WHY did I insist on clinging to this case until the last possible second? I did not know. The last wisps of mog remaining in my mind concealed my motives from me. There was something that did not want to be seen, but that must be seen before I could be a fully functioning Psych Doc. A true Psych Doc had no subconscious: anything in his mind could, when the occasion demanded, be brought to the surface quickly and easily.

Why did I not admit defeat gracefully, turn the case over to Jumo, and continue my training? Clearly, since my patient was not getting better, I needed to learn something more. Yet there was compulsion driving me, and I gave in to it. I told myself, *Sometimes there's hidden wisdom in a compulsion.*

After lunch I walked slowly from the cafe to Marge's hut, deep in thought. Karina met me in the doorway.

"Any change?" I asked.

She shook her head sadly. "None."

"I'll take over this shift."

"Okay. I'll be off duty this afternoon. If you have any trouble, yell for Jumo."

"Right."

She passed me. I turned to watch her cross the yard, her feet kicking up little puffs of dust. I couldn't help but feel a twinge of jealousy. Karina was so much younger than I, yet she was a full Psych Doc. She must have gotten her title when still in her teens. Probably it was easier when you're that young. You have less to unlearn.

I stepped into the hut.

Marge was in a different position. She now sat on the edge of the bed with her bare feet touching the floor. I glanced at her missing toe, but did not allow myself to stare at it. Had Karina moved Marge into this new position, or had Marge moved herself? It seemed unlikely Marge had moved herself. Karina would have mentioned that, since it might be a hopeful indication.

There was something Egyptian in the way Marge was sitting, legs together, hands in lap, gray clothing draped gracefully around her. Her head was pointed exactly straight ahead, making her look all the more like some Isis statue in a pharaoh's tomb. Her eyes were unfocused as ever, her face expressionless. I stood, looking into that empty face, for some time before speaking.

"Marge?"

There was not the slightest ghost of a reaction.

"Marge, you know you're actually lucky to be here. Places like this are called 'Decision Points.' There's a decision you can make right now, and you have three

Then Beggars Could Ride

main choices. First, you could decide to use your time here to think about what you actually want from life, what you want to do, what you want to be, even who you want to be. You can pick a new name, a new place to live, a new era, a new social role. The techs will train you for any life you choose and find a place for you in some enclave that suits you as well as is humanly possible.

"Second, if you don't want that, then, when you choose your new name, you can join the techs. I chose my new name and joined the techs all on the same day, and now I'm an apprentice psych tech. If you joined the techs there are thousands of jobs you could train for. It's a hard life with few rewards, but for some people—perhaps you're one—the important thing is to feel useful. There's no sexual discrimination, no obstacles to your promotion if you work hard and use judgment." I paused, watching for some reaction. There was none.

I did not want to talk about the third choice, but I had to be honest.

"Listen carefully, Marge, to the third choice. This is important. The techs are not sentimental about the life of individuals. Their interest is in society as a whole. If you insisted on remaining totally dependent, taking everything from society and giving nothing, you would be like a sick plant in their garden. Marge, sick plants are pulled up by the roots and destroyed." My voice was shaking. "Don't you understand? Someone—perhaps Jumo, perhaps Karina, perhaps myself—will put a gun to your head and shoot you."

It was impossible to know if she'd heard me or not.

Her face was as blank as ever.

"Marge, I may not like it, but I can't stop them. Nobody can stop them. They've set up the world so nobody else has more power, so only they have the full use of modern technology. You can't play mad girl forever. They set a time limit to such things, and *they can do as they please*." I felt like going down on my knees to her, begging her to listen. "I can understand how you might want to take a vacation from reality. I can understand how you might not want to ever come back. Once I tried to check out of this planet myself, so you can see I haven't always loved life in the enclaves. I've come to understand, though, that it's the best mere humans can do, the best they've ever done. I'm ready to do whatever must be done to maintain and protect it. Shakespeare knew 'All the world's a stage and all the men and women merely players.' It remained for our century to build on this insight the most gigantic stage production the human mind could conceive, using literally all the world and all the men and women in it. There's a play going on twenty-four hours a day, and there's a role in it for you, Marge. Somewhere there's a role for you. You think Cole Porter was the cat's pajamas? You ain't seen nothin' yet!"

She turned her head toward me, ever so slightly.

It probably meant nothing, I thought, but I took it as a sign to redouble my efforts.

"You've played roles before, Marge. Not just in Cole Porter musicals. You played a role with your first husband, this fellow Newton. You were his tormentor! And you forced a role on him, too. You forced him into the role of a helpless drunk! You and your mother practically pumped the alcohol down his throat! Of course, these things work both ways. Jumo has often pointed out—"

Abruptly I stopped. I thought, *I don't want to get into this.* The mog seemed suddenly to swirl up like swarm of angry bees.

But as Jumo had also pointed out, my tech training was deeply ingrained, almost a reflex. It was carrying me forward against my will straight toward the humming mog. I said, "Jumo has often pointed out that role projection works two ways. If you forced a role of helplessness on this Newton fellow, he was forcing the role of tormentor onto you. He was training you to be his demon, his evil ruler, his temptation." My eyes were filling with tears, but my tech logic carried me relentlessly deeper into the mog. "He was making a monster out of you so that whatever he did, he could say you drove him to it. And you were a good student! You became such a monster he couldn't stand you any more, nor could anyone else!" Through my tears I could still vaguely make out her mutilated foot. "Your poor little foot! Your poor little foot! I'm sorry—"

Without warning, she spoke, her voice harsh, full of amazement. *"You're Newton!"*

I stumbled backward, away from her, saying, "I'm Paul Rivers."

Now there was doubt in her voice, "But you're Newton, too, aren't you? Aren't you?"

"I'll discuss this with you later, Mrs. Patroni. Now

Then Beggars Could Ride

you must rest. I have to report this breakthrough to my superiors." My tech reflexes were still grinding away.

"If you're not Newton, how do you know so much about him?" she demanded. My vision had cleared enough so I could see her face. It had come completely to life. Her eyes were the old Marge eyes I remembered, suspicious, accusing.

I did not run, though I felt like running.

I walked stiff-legged out into the dusty sun-drenched roadway.

I shouted, "Jumo! Doc Jumo! Come quick!"

The mog whirled around me, faster and faster. It had not been dead, only sleeping.

CHAPTER 19

Jumo and I stood on the cliff, watching the shadow of our mountain creep over the face of Mexico City, over the beehive pattern of enclaves where lights winked on in distant windows. As evening came, the wind picked up, but it blew hot, not cool. The night would probably be as sweltering as the day. We could hear the city, but no separate sounds. It hummed, as my head hummed. Everything was so perfectly organized down there. A place for everyone and everyone in his place, and if one or two didn't fit, there were donkeys to bring them up the mountain to us.

I asked, "How is Marge?"

Jumo answered quietly, "Excellent. I have her under sedation, though. She'll sleep better that way."

"And tomorrow?"

"If this case follows the course I expect, she will be a little unstable tomorrow, but I doubt if she'll relapse. We'll have to be careful as she starts eating. It will be a while before her stomach is fully open for business."

"Her stomach!" I said impatiently. "It's her mind I'm worried about. What am I going to tell her?"

"About you being Newton?"

"What else?"

"She's your patient. I'm putting you in full charge of her again, since you seem to be making progress at last. So it's your decision what you tell her."

"I don't understand how, of all the people in the world who might end up with her case, it had to be me. Why me? I mean, it's an impossible coincidence."

Jumo smiled. "It's not a coincidence."

"What do you mean?"

"I arranged it. You see, this therapy is not for her alone. It's also for you."

I shook my head violently, trying to get rid of the humming mog. "If that's true, I don't think much of your treatment. It's making me worse, not better."

"You're having mog trouble?"

"Horrible mog trouble! And I thought it was almost gone."

"It will go when you have no more unfinished business.

Then Beggars Could Ride

And so far as I know, Marge is the last of your serious unfinished business."

"Will it clear up if I tell Marge the truth?"

"It will clear up when you tell yourself the truth. That's what mog is, you know: lies, and unmade decisions, and unfaced facts. It's part of you hiding from the rest behind a smokescreen. Most people seem to feel they can't live without mog, but it's one of many luxuries the psych tech can't afford." He gestured toward the city below where more and more lights were appearing. "Those people down there sometimes dream of revolt. They can steal our weapons, learn to use our technology. Of course they can! But our truly decisive weapon they cannot steal: we see more clearly than they do. Remember Leonardo DaVinci's slogan? 'Only the trained eye really sees.' All that you have done since you first came in contact with us, all that you are doing now, all that you will ever do in the psych techs, is directed toward giving you that tiny little edge, clear vision."

My own vision, at least my interior vision, was far from clear. I said miserably, "Before I get that clear vision, how can I tell what is truth and what isn't?"

He laid his hand on my shoulder. "Do the best you can. If you fail, learn from your failure." He started back toward the village. His face was in shadow so I could not see his expression. "Tomorrow morning talk to her again." These words were softly spoken, but had the hard certainty of a command.

I OBSERVED my breakfast, but did not eat it.

Karina, sitting next to me in the cafe, was worried about me. "You're doing fine," she said, and squeezed my hand. "And your Jill is doing fine, too."

One of the night crew called over, "She drank orange juice this morning, and held the glass in her own hand."

I thought, *Marge is awake already.* A nasty surprise.

I thought, *You have to get up pretty early in the morning to fool old Marge.*

I pushed back my chair and stood up. I was tired. I was groggy. I swayed as if drunk. I muttered, "I'd better go and see her."

Karina was frowning up at me. I was surprised to see she cared about me, was concerned about my welfare. But then, Karina was a psych tech. It was her job to be concerned about people. I wasn't a psych tech. I wasn't a Doc. Maybe I never would be one. *That's right,* said the mog.

I shuffled out into the early morning sunlight.

The huts were white. The sky was blue. There were no clouds. People passed me as I walked along. Some of them waved. Some didn't.

I walked on grass when I could. It felt better on my bare feet. The air was cooler than last night, but it would warm up by noon.

I knew one thing, the reason I'd refused to quit Marge's case. I loved her. It was horrible but true. I loved her. I had always loved her, but all the games got in the way. It wasn't that I needed to own her, to chase off all the other males. That love was dead. This was a new love. This was a love that came from seeing her clearly in my mind, and seeing miracles in her. I had never, until this morning, actually looked at her. She was, when I didn't hide her from myself with those masks that made her my enemy, a good, simple, courageous woman, a strong, supportive partner, a very clever and tough and wise broad, if a bit naive. I wanted good things for her, perhaps with me, but if not with me with someone else who would treat her right.

I mean, she deserved something good. She'd paid her dues, with interest.

If she started in with the old games, I'd say, "None of that," and she'd quit.

"Oh, yeah?" said the mog.

I hesitated outside her door before going in. I took off my broad-brimmed straw hat and held it to my chest, knowing I must look like a cartoonist's idea of a Mexican peasant.

"Hello, Marge," I said, stepping through the doorway.

She sat up in bed. I could see she was weak, but her eyes were alert, her face mobile. "Ah, Mr. Rivers, I believe. I'm afraid I've put you and everyone else around here to an awful lot of trouble." She was wearing a loose-fitting white hospital smock. "I had a delusion that you were my ex-husband. I hope you'll forgive me."

I took a step forward. "It wasn't a delusion, Marge."

She looked at me a long time in silence, not moving. Gradually a feeling of horror came over me. Was she slipping back into catatonia? Was this too much for her?

"Marge!" I called out sharply.

She smiled. "I'm all right. Actually it's a relief." She sighed. "Yes, damnit. It's a relief. I'm not crazy after all."

"No, you're not, thank God."

We both laughed.

She said, "Come sit on my bed and tell me all you've been doing since I saw you last." She patted the bedspread with her feeble hand. I sat down and began.

Never before had it been so easy to talk to her.

WHEN she was strong enough she moved to my hut, and there I nursed her patiently back to full health. What can I say? It all happened so naturally. I don't remember when we began making love. That came naturally, too. But the games, the evil games we used to play to hurt each other, did not recommence.

A year passed.

The mog had vanished, never to return.

Marge had begun working with the patients.

One morning, slightly before noon, Jumo, Marge and I stood on the cliff, looking out over the shimmering city.

Marge said, "Jumo, could I become a psych tech?"

He answered, "If you're willing to work and wait. It takes a while sometimes, isn't that right, Doc Rivers?"

He used my full title in that manner only occasionally, with a note of fondness and irony. I was a full-fledged Doc to everyone but him; to him I would always be, in a way, his special student.

"I'd like to start as soon as possible," said Marge firmly.

"You already have started," he said. "But there are formal things you should learn. Karina can teach you the elementary mental exercises."

She gave him a quick kiss on the cheek. "Thanks, Jumo!"

After lunch Marge and I did not go immediately to our separate tasks, but lingered a while, standing silent together, staring at things. The noonday sun beat down relentlessly on the squalid and decaying whitewashed huts of paradise.

www.ingramcontent.com/pod-product-compliance
Ingram Content Group UK Ltd.
Pitfield, Milton Keynes, MK11 3LW, UK
UKHW041957230426

12048UKWH00008B/389